Exile

by

Rachel Stern

DORRANCE PUBLISHING CO., INC.
PITTSBURGH, PENNSYLVANIA 15222

All Rights Reserved
Copyright © 1998 by Rachel Stern
No part of this book may be reproduced or transmitted
in any form or by any means, electronic or mechanical,
including photocopying, recording, or by any information
storage and retrieval system without permission
in writing from the publisher.

ISBN # 0-8059-3724-2
Printed in the United States of America

First Printing

For information or to order additional books, please write:
Dorrance Publishing Co., Inc.
643 Smithfield Street
Pittsburgh, Pennsylvania 15222
U.S.A.
Or visit our web site and on-line catalog at *www.dorrancepublishing.com*

Dedication

To the memory of the nameless bards of Israel
and the singing men and women who followed them.

Contents

	Author's Note vii
	Character List ix
Chapter 1	The Departure 1
Chapter 2	The Journey 6
Chapter 3	The Reception 11
Chapter 4	The Settlement 18
Chapter 5	Lily 24
Chapter 6	Neziah 28
Chapter 7	Jeduthun 35
Chapter 8	By the Rivers of Babylon 43
Chapter 9	Ethan 48
Chapter 10	Marriages 52
Chapter 11	Scholars 61
Chapter 12	Naarah and Ethan 66
Chapter 13	Lily and Neziah 72
Chapter 14	The Nile 80
Chapter 15	Jarib 85
Chapter 16	The Lyre 89
Chapter 17	The Widow 97
Chapter 18	The Loom 101
Chapter 19	Bread upon the Water 107
Chapter 20	The Chest 111
	Epilogue 115

Author's Note

This is a midrash: a story that might have been.

It grew out of my enduring love of the Psalms and my concern at the skittish way in which Christians handle the development of the canons.

The Psalms were the musical bridge between Judaism and Christianity. Might they not have also been the bond that held the Jews of the captivity together and brought them home?

Since almost nothing is reliably known of what went on in the Jewish communities during the seventy years of exile, I have dared imagine a family who experienced that pivotal time. I say pivotal because scholars do agree on two things: the Jews returned as firm monotheists, cured of their lingering polytheism; and in Babylon they developed the synagogue system, which is prevalent today.

Of my theologian friends who quailed at my temerity, I beg indulgence. And I thank them and many others for their gracious help.

Rachel Stern
1995

Character List

The household of Jeduthun, who came in the second deportation:

    Jeduthun, musician and singer
    Lily, his daughter
    Ethan, Lily's son
    Jarib, Lily's first husband; father of Ethan
    Tamar, female servant
    Atab, male servant

Eleazar, a priest

The household of Hanan, who came in the first deportation:
    Hanan, prince of Judah, merchant
    Neziah ben Hanan, his son
    Ullah, Neziah's wife
    Azaz, their son
    Teman, their son
    Bunah, steward of family residential property
    Gomer, Neziah's body servant
    Likhi, accountant at Hanan warehouse
    Adah, a maid

Amok, a spy

The household of Ethan
    Ethan, noted singer, grandson of Jeduthun
    Naarah, coloratura, wife of Ethan, daughter of Likhi
    Jadah, Naarah's grandmother
    Shama, son of Ethan and Naarah
    Sabta, son of Ethan and Naarah
    Alhai, daughter of Ethan and Naarah
    Eber, husband of Alhai
    Darda, oldest son of Alhai and Eber

Rachel Stern

    Arissi, a Babylonian woman of the nobility
    Adelia, her daughter

    Amanu, a Babylonian weaver

    Zelzah, an Ethiopian captive

    Diklah, a Jewish widow

Chapter 1
The Departure

The man lay upon his face in an agony of prayer. It was his last act of worship in the Temple, the dwelling place of the Most High, whose wrath would delay no longer. On the morrow, Jerusalem would become the spoil of the army of Nebuchadnezzar, and the remaining sons of Jacob would be driven captive to the "Land Between The Rivers."

"How then can Thy priests offer morning and evening burnt sacrifices to Thy glory?" the man's lips moved in a whisper. "How then can Thy musicians prophesy and offer sacrifices of praise and thanksgiving? How long will Thy chosen suffer at the hands of evil men? Save, Lord, for Thy name's sake."

At first light, Jeduthun drew himself up to his full height, a fine figure of a man in his prime, bearded and deep-chested. He faced squarely the Holy of Holies and his vibrant baritone gave utterance to one of the oldest songs in The Praises of Israel, attributed to David when he brought the ark from Hebron and ordered his choirs. From Jeduthun s well-taught memory came the ancient words, now at the end as at the beginning:

> "... *Save us, O God of our salvation, and gather us together, and deliver us from the heathen, that we may give thanks to Thy holy name and glory to Thy praise. Blessed be the Lord God of Israel for ever and eve...*"[1]

Hastening down the steps, the master singer was accosted by an old and withered priest.

"Jeduthun, my son, take these," the venerable one said and handed him an armload of scrolls.

"Yes, yes. Let us go. We must make haste."

"No, I cannot make such a journey. It is for you, our chief musician, to carry on the heritage and keep the faith. Let not the memory fail."

Jeduthun bowed his head for a blessing:

"The Lord God be your strength, Rejoice in the God of Israel, our salvation."

The two men went their separate ways—the old priest to the murky recesses of the Temple, Jeduthun to join his family at the gate of Benjamin. Both felt the bitter impossibility of rejoicing in the Lord.

Rachel Stern

The musician found his family, a group of four in the midst of hundreds, awaiting their turn to be expelled from Jerusalem and herded to Babylon on this the third day of the second deportation of Judah.

There they were. His daughter Lily, hardly more than a child herself, was the mother of the merry boy Ethan, age three. Tamar, the serving woman, had brought up Lily after the death of her mother and was still in full charge of household matters. It was Tamar who had found Atab to do the heavy work and was now, at last, proving useful in handling the donkey. They had evidently just arrived at the gate, for both Atab and the donkey were breathing heavily and Atab was cursing the beast.

"Quiet, here comes the master," said Tamar.

"Here, take these carefully! Put them in the chest. They are valuable."

Jeduthun gave the order and pushed past toward the soldier in command of the gate.

"But the chest is full..." Lily's voice was weak.

"Make space for the scrolls, woman."

Jeduthun thrust his way through the milling, wailing Jews to the captain of the Babylonian guard, who was standing between two spear men on a small platform near the wall.

"I am Jeduthun, chief musician and singer of the temple. I have with me a party of four..."

"You will meet your betters with the musicians of Babylon." The captain curled his lips, and Jeduthun's jaw muscles twitched. "Present yourself to the scribe there." The captain pointed to a scribe seated at a table, back to wall, surrounded by impatient, angry Jews kept at bay by the spearmen.

Jeduthun strode to the scribe, his respectful countrymen making way for him.

"Jeduthun, chief musician. A party of four including a child."

The scribe wrote this twice on a leather strap which he cut in two. He tossed one half into a reed basket; the other half he gave to Jeduthun.

Jeduthun examined his passport to captivity. It was written not only in duplicate but in two languages, the cuneiform of the conquerors and the classic Hebrew of the conquered. Without this identity tag, he would be prey to every Moabite and Edomite bandit along the trail. Without this deportation card his family would be victims of the pillaging army occupying the Holy City—Pigs! Infidels!

He suppressed his rage and rejoined his sad little group around the cart. His daughter wiped tears as she unpacked the chest. Her wedding finery was on the ground. Lutes, harps, and horns lay about, but the four precious scrolls were in. Tamar was studying the most efficient arrangement for the instruments. She placed them, the larger to the bottom, a lyre and a hand harp on top. The lid would not fit; the fragile wood of sound boxes could be crushed. Lily removed the lyre and the harp. There

Exile

was no space for her carefully-woven garments with their embroidered trimmings. Weeping silently, she shook out the dust and bundled them for hand carrying. Jeduthun picked up his lyre and his harp and examined them.

Would they survive the fateful journey? Could he and his people stand the hardships of the stony desert? Could they live through days and months of walking ever deeper into the maw of Jehovah's enemies and Israel's conquerors? "Why did He allow this?"

His bitter reverie was broken by a cry from Lily—"Where is Ethan? Where is my little son? Ethan! Ethan!"

Tamar and Atab sprang up and joined the distracted mother in her search. They were glad of any excuse to leave their particular pocket of sadness and mingle with the crowd. But they could not see Ethan, such a small mite. Suddenly a knot of youngsters broke into a scuffle and the least of them broke into a bawl, "Mama."

Lily ran up and rescued the cause of the disturbance. "Now, now, darling."

"They pushed me over. They won't let me..."

"He's ruining our game. He's a baby pest..."

Ethan clung to his mother, refusing to stand on his fat legs. And so the slight, young woman carried him back to the cart and to the stately grandfather, who had been obliged to hold the cursed donkey in place.

"Ethan, Ethan, why do you worry us so?"

But Ethan was eager to change the subject. He said, "Grandfather, when are we going to Babylon? Let's go!"

Tamar found one of Atab's leather straps, looped it around Ethan's chest and tied him to a shaft. Ethan roared in outrage, but even his mother turned a cold eye. Soon he sat down, then lay down, then fell asleep.

So the family huddled until noon. Tamar reached into a basket and gave each a single wheat cake.

"Must we start starving so soon?" Jeduthun was used to good food and plenty of it, good treatment and even pampering. His position in Jerusalem commanded it.

Without the least mark of respect, a soldier yelled his name. And the family got into motion toward the gate. They passed through and found themselves in company with five other families under the charge of one officer and two subordinates.

The officer, in shining helmet with feathered crest, led the way on horseback. He was disappointed both in his horse and in his job—his army friends back in the city would have all the glory and the loot. With him were two foot soldiers, one on each side of the file of deported Jews. They watched and walked while the officer rode and occasionally circled to keep the deportees from straying or straggling.

So, the family of Jeduthun—his daughter Lily, his grandson Ethan, his maid servant Tamar, and his man servant Atab—found themselves in line with some dozen other families walking away from their home and their city toward the abominable land of their oppressors. They looked about at their fellow citizens and did not see a familiar face. Jeduthun's life had been entirely devoted to the music of the Temple, preparation and presentation of the praises of Israel to the one, eternal and true God of their fathers. His household who served him had no time for gadding or interest in idle gossip with their neighbors. In their proud isolation, they accepted the fact that there were no other musicians at hand. No priests either. Jeduthun's family would naturally set the tone.

At sunset they halted for the night. Tamar, like all the other women, went into her jars and bags of prepared food and brought forth a meager ration of dried goat meat and baked bread. Lily went down to the river and brought up a jar of water. They ate in silence. Even Ethan was too tired to fuss. Atab opened up a large goat hair cloth and stretched it from the cart to poles, thereby creating the privacy of a tent for the women. Jeduthun and the manservant unrolled their bedding of hides and stretched out under the stars.

All about them people were trying to settle to sleep, but there was a restlessness heard in the broken yet continual sounds of distress. Jeduthun felt the restlessness, too. He knew that this fatal day needed a benediction. These people needed to unburden their hearts and their hands and lay hold on the steadfast love of God.

He reached for his harp and stood up, searching his memory for fitting words and music. He would cobble something together to feed the abandoned sheep of Judah. A whisper spread, "Jeduthun will sing."

A few sweeps of the harp strings introduced the chief musician's vibrant baritone and he stood in the midst of his people as if before them and their God in the Temple court. He faced their lost city; as he sang they, too, looked back.

> "*Great is the Lord, and greatly to be praised in the city of our God, in the mountain of His holiness.*
> *Beautiful for situation, the joy of the whole earth, is Mount Zion, on the sides of the north, the city of the great King.*
> *God is known in her palaces for a refuge.*
> *Walk about Zion, and go round about her: count the towers thereof.*
> *Mark ye well her bulwarks, consider her palaces; that He may tell it to the generations to come.*"[2]

He sang tenderly, like a lover. He paused and played a harp interlude sweetly while the people remembered Jerusalem.

Suddenly Jeduthun's voice burst forth in agony:

Exile

> "O God, hast Thou cast us off forever? Why doesn't Thine anger smoke against the sheep of Thy pasture?
>
> "Remember Thy congregation, which Thou hast purchased of old: the rod of throe inheritance, which Thou hast redeemed: this Mount Zion, wherein Thou has dwelt.
>
> O Lord God of hosts, how long wilt Thou be angry against the prayer of Thy people?
>
> Thou feedest them with the bread of tears; and givest them tears to drink in great measure.
>
> Let the singing of the prisoners come before Thee; according to the greatness of Thy power, preserve Thou those that are appointed to die."[3]

Again Jeduthun paused and let his harp accompany the wails of the people:

> "How long, O Lord, how long this woe?"

Then confidently the soloist raised his arms and from deep within brought forth the poem of trust:

> "...We will not go back from Thee: quicken us and we will call upon Thy name.
>
> Turn us again, O Lord God of hosts, cause Thy face to shine; and we shall be saved."[4]

The people bowed in silent, healing prayer. Jeduthun had settled upon his hard place on the ground and was dozing when a warm, fat, little boy nestled himself into his arms and said, "They told me to sleep with you. Mama's sick."

Jeduthun held his grandson against his shoulder. This little child, Ethan, was the apple of his eye, though he would not admit it even to himself.

"Well, now, what ails your mother?"

"She's sick. They told me to go to you. Will you sing to me? I heard you. It was beautiful."

So the mighty voice was brought down to a whisper and Jeduthun sang a lullaby for the small boy. And the boy fell asleep amid visions of guardian angels watching over him.

---

[1] Chronicles 16
[2] Psalms 48, 12
[3] Psalms 74, 79, 80
[4] Psalms 80

Chapter 2
The Journey

Early next morning Jeduthun awakened to a chirping little melody:

> *"We are going to Babylon, Babylon.*
> *Let's get going to Babylon, Babylon.*
> *Oh, ho Babylon! Babylon, Bab-bab-Babylon*
> *That's where we're going today—"*

He smiled to hear his grandson's voice, opened his eyes and saw the plump imp relieving himself too close for comfort. He jumped up and went to the women's tent to see what all the stir had been about during the night. Tamar greeted him with a finger to her lips.

"She is sleeping at last. It was stillborn. A very small, male child."

Lily lay whiter than new ivory upon a rumpled pallet. Her hair was matted and her body seemed thinner than ever under the mass of it. Jeduthun looked down helplessly.

He followed Tamar to the back of the cart from which she was handing out a meager ration from their pitiably small store. There was not much food to be had during the siege, and they would not have had any at all except for gifts from the Temple. Tamar was aware of their good fortune, as were they all, and thankful. What she also knew and marveled at was that none of the other departing families had brought servants. How could gentle folk manage without?

As if to make the point, Atab returned with the half-shovel. He had been covering the night soil and burying the issue of Lily's brief travail.

They were eating quietly when a soldier came up bawling, "Make haste! Pack up! Get going."

Jeduthun glared at him. "We have a sick woman here. She can't move."

The soldier snorted, "Well, leave her. I'll take care of any stray girls. Ha-ha."

Jeduthun would have knocked his teeth in, but the bully turned away quickly. His orders were to get those Jews to Babylonia without incident, as if it were possible to have a bunch of Jews without trouble. Orders were orders.

Exile

They finally got on the road, each buried in his own thoughts and private griefs. Only Ethan danced about, wanted to ride in the cart with mama, wanted to ride on grandpa's shoulders, wanted to ride on Atab's back "like a horsey." As the sun rose higher in blasting heat, even he gave up and sat down. "Where is Babylon?" he whimpered. Lily took him into the cart with her, while the donkey balked at every step.

Jeduthun had to adjust his stride to the pace of his family and of the whole herd of Judeans. He was bitter about this second deportation. One wretched king had cost them all of their top people; a second foolish king was wrenching from the land the backbone of the race; only toilers were left. Their wealth of court and Temple had already gone ahead to enrich the conquerors. Jeremiah had been right from the beginning. Now even he had gone down into Egypt, perfidious Egypt, like Lily's husband.

And Lily, weak and jolted in the cart, thought bitterly of her husband Jarib. He had bribed his way through the encircling army and tried to persuade the family to slip out the way he came. He had argued in vain, for Jeduthun remembered good King Hezekiah who put his trust in Jehovah and had seen the Assyrian forces melt away.

"Stay then. I'll see you in Babylon. I'll have an hour with my wife." He was so young and foolish.

Jarib had stormed into Lily's room, had thrown her on the bed and had done his husbandly act on her with great pumping and blowing.

"Go with me, wife. I have a caravan just beyond the ridge."

Lily could only weep and plead that her baby son was safer in the city of God, that her father knew best. He had taken her again. Pulling away he had patted her flat belly and said, "I'll have another son when I join you in the Land Between The Rivers."

She remembered this in her weakness, and for the first time she felt a spark of rebellion. "It isn't fair!"

She had always submitted to her husband's conjugal demands without complaint, though he gave her no pleasure in bed. Childbearing was the crowning joy for the wife, but what if the man ran off to his business and left the woman with the heavy work of packing and loading for departure? And what if the child came too soon in a crimson flood? Jarib should not have left her with child. He thought only of himself. "Marriage isn't fair."

They were walking through Samaria, Jeduthun told them. The word stirred Tamar's memory: stories told by her grandparents, stories the grandparents had heard from their elders. The Northern Kingdom, once Israel, had been destroyed by the Assyrian conqueror and the ten tribes of that region had been driven into exile between the rivers. Tamar's own forebears, poor farmers, were left to till the soil until pushed out by alien people whom the Assyrians sent west to stabilize the region. Tamar recalled the hardships and desperation that drove her own parents south to the surviving Southern

Kingdom. Only two tribes then remained, Judah and Benjamin, but they held the glorious city of David and the Temple of King Solomon. Tamar and her kin were glad to find work there. And now this. It was too much. She was walking through the old country and could not even understand the language of the mixed breeds that stood or ran along the road. It was just as well, for all the jeers and taunts, being in Aramaic, failed to hurt the Judeans.

Atab, a simple fellow, had his hands full keeping the load on the cart and the donkey in motion. He admired the soldiers, stuck his tongue out at the tormentors, and endured. Food and drink were all he wanted.

As the sun lowered in the west, the military escort brought the deportees to a halt. The Judeans made camp as best they could, ate of their meager stores, and sank wearily to rest. Jeduthun lay on his back, looking at the stars—God's handiwork. The eastern heathen presumed to know all about stars and called this knowledge wisdom. Well, they were wise enough to beat the king of Judea.

Jeduthun was trying to calm his churning mind when a neighbor touched him and said, "Maestro, sing for us. We need the praises of Israel this night."

Jeduthun felt the need, too, and so he rose and stroked his harp. In clear, ringing tones he invoked the Deity:

> *"Hear me when 1 call, O God of my righteousness: Thou hast enlarged me when 1 was in distress; have mercy upon me, and hear my prayer."*[5]

Jeduthun paused. His listeners waited for the answer. It came from deep within the broad breast of the singer, low and awesome like the roll of distant thunder:

> *"O ye sons of men, how long will ye turn My glory into shame? How long will ye love vanity, and seek after falsehood?"*

Again the psalmist paused. His listeners felt individual flickerings of conscience. Some felt guilt for tithes withheld, strangers turned away; others recalled sharp deals, or envy and strife—all because they loved their wealth more than they loved their Lord. A few sensed that the prophets had warned rightly, that the totality of personal sin had tainted the whole nation and brought on the wrath of God. The lying and cheating that marked their dealings with people had reached unto their relations with God. Their righteous God was justly angry. They fell on their face and moaned: "O Lord, have mercy on us."

Jeduthun took up again the time-honored song, handed down from David's music:

> "But know that God has set apart him that is godly for Himself: the Lord will hear when I call to Him."[7]

And again came the deep and awesome tones like distant thunder:

> "Stand in awe and sin not; commune with your own heart upon your bed, and be still. Offer the sacrifices of righteousness and put your trust in the Lord."[8]

Jeduthun's harp interlude gave time for reflection before he resumed the psalm:

> "There be many that say, Who will show us any good?
> Lord, lift Thou up the light of Thy countenance upon us.
> I will both lay me down in peace, and sleep: For Thou Lord only maketh me dwell in safety."[9]

Day followed night, and they walked. Night followed day and they camped. It seemed an endless repetition under worsening conditions. Food ran low; sandals wore out. Fatigue and sickness reduced them. They walked, stumbled, and dragged over a barren waste of endless sand, under the pitiless sun, burning and blinding.

The Judeans had been turned away from Damascus with its springs and tall palms heavy with dates. Their track, kept for the military and royal messengers, bent eastward, the shortest route between the Euphrates and the Western Sea. Its shallow arc through the desert was defined by some half dozen oases guarded by soldiers. From these came carts carrying meager rations of dried peas, dates, and water.

The family of Jeduthun stumbled to a halt at the second watering place. They looked at each other in despair. Their skin was begrimed; their clothing ragged and stiff with dirt; their eyes, sunken in skeletal sockets, seemed bigger than ever. Little Ethan had lost his baby fat and his bounce; he lay in Lily's arms sucking his thumb. The four adults had been pulling the cart since the donkey died. They traded his hide to a sutler for two loaves of bread and a skin of water. Tamar, who did all the bartering, knew she had been cheated, but it was the best she could do. It was the same with Lily's finery. Even the skins on which they slept had been cut up to bind their lacerated feet. But the contents of the chest—scrolls and musical instruments of great beauty and price—had not been touched. When Tamar would reproach her master about this, he would say, "Though we perish, they must not. They are our heritage."

At this desperate point in their endless journey, Tamar did not ask permission. She snatched Jeduthun's zither in a moment when he was distracted by a fit of coughing. When night came, she went into the settlement to see what she could do. Jeduthun would not miss the zither, for his head and lungs were so congested by dust that he had not been able to sing for a week. Besides, the wheels of the cart were so cracked and broken that they could not carry the chest. And how could their heritage survive if they did not?

Tamar quickly found a group of men singing around a well. With signs and a few words she had picked up in the course of her dealings, she made known that the zither was to be had for a pair of runners to replace the wheels of the cart, turning it into a sort of sled. So it was that the next morning a carpenter came and did the work. His employer, a singing soldier, went off with the zither. Jeduthun coughed and wept but said nothing. He was relieved that he had not been forced to make the decision.

They picked up the shafts of the once-cart, now sled, and dragged on. And on, with no end in sight. Cut and bruised feet gave full meaning to the words "foot sore." Chronic fatigue silenced them. And they dropped down, wearier each night than the night before. But they traded only one more valuable—the harp—and that again for food and water to supplement the starvation allotments regularly provided by the Babylonian army.

As they were approaching the last watering place, two men on horseback, leading camels, came riding along the lines of exiles.

"We seek Jeduthun, the chief musician of the Temple. Where is he?"

"Jeduthun, the singer. Point him out."

And so Jeduthun was found. The horsemen dismounted and bowed low before the gaunt, filthy wreck of a man.

"Maestro, our master Hanan, a prince of Judah, salutes you and asks the honor of your company in his home. We have provisions and mounts at your service."

Jeduthun drew himself up to his full height and wheezed, "We are honored to accept. We thank your princely master."

The horseman made the camels kneel and helped the exhausted people into carry-alls, one on either side of each came. The passengers were too stunned by their sudden good fortune to notice the intricate basket work of their carriages or the smooth pace of the camels. They felt only relief at the end of their journey and thanks to God for Jewish hospitality.

---

[5] Psalms 4
[6] Psalms 4
[7] Psalms 4
[8] Psalms 4
[9] Psalms 4

Chapter 3
The Reception

Hanan's house stood by the river in the midst of smaller buildings, making a sort of compound. The family of Jeduthun was brought into a guest house, whose thick walls kept out the heat and gave the exhausted newcomers the first comfort they had felt in months.

Nourishing broths, cool baths, and clean clothing were promptly provided. A doctor came, left ungents and orders. The five worn travelers slept and slept, rousing themselves only long enough to accept treatment from kind and ministering hands.

Jeduthun awoke one morning in full possession of his faculties and surveyed the situation. He and Atab lay in one room permeated by the odor of pitch. He assumed that the other three lay in another and got up to see. His door led into a vestibule from which the women's quarters branched. He quickly said, "Good day and God bless," and modestly closed their door. Turning, he saw the physician and greeted him with thanks.

The doctor smiled and said, "It is my privilege to heal all the sick and sore. But now, Jeduthun, we must restore your voice." He placed his hand on the singer" diaphragm. "The voice. That is the important thing. So listen carefully and follow exactly the regimen I shall prescribe for you:

"Do not speak above a whisper. Do not exert yourself. Three times a day and once at night you must go into the closed cubicle in which precious benzoin is burning. Breathe deeply there. Otherwise rest your lungs and stay within the tar vapor. It soothes throat and nasal passages. I have informed Hanan and his servants."

Jeduthun started to speak, but the doctor put finger to lips and departing said, "We must save the voice. Yes?"

The little family began to regain their good looks. They ate and rested. They bathed in water and were rubbed with oil. Their hair shone and their feet once again could spring. Ethan was the first to recover. Though he had lost all his baby fat, he began to regain it and he ran about on stout little legs. Lily was languid. Her former beauty returned, however: glossy braids, full mouth, no longer pinched. The two servants thoroughly enjoyed being waited on and cosseted. Atab stayed the longest abed. Always, the pitch bubbled over a brazier in their rooms, a relief from the dust.

A week passed. The steward of Hanan's household came to bid Jeduthun to dine with his host. A servant followed bearing rich apparel and a copper mirror.

"Perhaps the maestro would like to adorn himself for the honor of the occasion."

Jeduthun did just that, and was pleased with what the mirror gave back to him: a tall, stately man, of deep chest and strong arms, a full curling beard clipped clean at his lips, mingling with black hair that came to his shoulders. His robe was a reddish brown, woven with squares and triangles of yellow. His feet were shod with yellow sandals. Most gorgeous of all was the purple girdle, Tyrean no doubt, that bound his waist.

He followed a servant through the compound, through a grove and a garden, to the main house and into the private apartments of the owner—Hanan, prince of Judah, merchant prince in Babylon. For the first time Jeduthun met his host, a tall, thin man with a white beard and thin sharp features, clad in loose raiment of bright blue and green. He raised himself with the help of an attendant and leaned on a cane.

"Welcome to our humble abode, most honorable musician. I'd have come to you sooner but, as you see, my knees are feeling their age. Even our good doctor says he cannot cure the ravages of time. I am delighted that he reports progress in your case. Come, sit beside me. I understand that you must still spare your voice."

The two sat on cushioned chairs. Servants brought in tables and savory dishes. Hanan ate sparingly and did most of the talking. Jeduthun ate heartily and whispered replies. He was amazed at his host's familiarity with the great ones of Israel and Babylonia and at the casual manner in which he spoke of them: Sennacherib, a butcher, ought to have had a stall in the market; Josiah, a well-meaning amateur who got himself killed; Jeremiah and all those silly prophets, always howling against the rich. What finally did happen to Jeremiah?

Most amazing was the way Hanan spoke of Nebuchednezzar, the great king bent on the destruction of the Jews. Jeduthun spat at the mention of that name but Hanan went on:

"My friend, don't be so bitter. We, or rather our destructive little kings, gave him ample provocation. If you look at the great city that he is building and the ancient landmarks he is restoring, you will find him a great architect—a man of vision, not a mere general. You will see the canals that water the fields and keep river's floods from doing harm. Go down to the river where you can see trading boats, barges laden with merchandise, which can move as far as the Eastern Sea. Here our conqueror keeps the confluence of the two rivers dug out in a channel so that great ships can bring freight, both rare and utilitarian."

Hanan saw that his guest knew nothing of trade and cared less. He turned the conversation to their families and said that his son was away on business, but that his daughter-in-law would call on Lily. He asked about

Exile

Jeduthun's plans for the future. Jeduthun said he hoped to make a living by singing and giving lessons.

"Ah, yes. The Babylonians love music and pay well. I can help you get started. Please come to dine with me again tomorrow. We shall talk further."

Jeduthun and Hanan had dinner together and talked freely for many days. In spite of the difference in their backgrounds and interest, they enjoyed each others' company, for each recognized in the other a man of pre-eminence in his field. They found excellence in one another and admired it.

In the course of these conversations, it was revealed that Hanan, driven out of Jerusalem with the first deportation some eleven years earlier, had landed on his feet because most of his trading posts were in far places, the biggest in Babylon.

With a laugh Hanan said, "Not home, but no hardship. We just settled in and made the best of what the Lord had provided. Prophets or no prophets, was it not God's will that we prospered? My son Neziah is out with a caravan now, and I assure you, he will not come back empty-handed. However," he sighed, "more and more I need him in the counting house and warehouses across the river. These old bones..."

Neziah's wife, Ullah, came to call on Lily at the command of her father-in-law. The meeting was not a success. Ullah wore a proud, fixed smile. Her lips spoke graciousness but her heart cried disdain. As innocent of worldly ways as Lily was, she felt the coldness and had difficulty keeping up her end of the conversation.

"My husband goes out with caravans, too. Now he is in Egypt."

"How interesting."

"Perhaps they have met."

"I doubt it."

Lily, whose only offense was to be beautiful, knew the direst social cut. It was as if the older woman had said, "A great merchant prince like my husband would never have occasion to speak to a mere camel driver like yours."

They parted in a flurry of polite, empty phrases.

But the companionable hours together continued to unite Hanan and Jeduthun. As the latter's health improved, the former made the suggestion that his guests stroll about the compound and see it as a working operation. "Almost self-supporting. We have to buy very little and it gives work to many of our countrymen who would otherwise be idling in mischief or making bricks for the Babylonians."

"Like our forefathers in Egypt," added Jeduthun.

"Or so we've been told. But I don't see any Moses around here," was Hanan's response.

And so his guests found themselves doing what they thought never to do again if they could help it: walking. In the cool light of early morning and the pink dusk of late afternoon, they walked and saw trees and gardens, a bake house, a cobbler's shop, a large weaving room, laundry pools, and a grainery. Interspersed were the small habitations of the busy Jews, kept employed by the House of Hanan.

Hanan's property included gardens and orchards in luxuriant growth; an Eden. Runnels of flowering water laced through the rich soil, and that water came from the life-giving river beyond. There was nothing like this great fertile plain in Palestine nor even a free trickle of water in the desert that lay between them and home. It was marvelous to behold.

The Euphrates, that great water, sprang from snowy peaks far to the north, carrying, in spring flood and mud, that which nourished a land of talented and energetic people. A twin stream, the Tigris, flowing south almost parallel, added its rich burden so that the region between the rivers in earliest times became a cradle of civilization. Here, abundance bred skills and cultures that spread through the "fertile crescents"... The gifted people—Sumarians, Babylonians, Assyrians—caught the spring floods in basins and canals, protecting themselves against floods and providing irrigation in a thirsty land. They connected the canals in a network of waterways that carried their commerce to market cities.

But the river was fickle: it changed course over time. When it did, it left the cities on its banks to decay. People moved with the traffic of commerce and abandoned their brick buildings which caved in, to become heaps or wells. The bricks were mud and they returned to mud. The river brought the mud to a land without stone, and the river took it away. Thousands of years of change lay behind the Euphrates and Babylon, the crowned city it buttressed.

Hanan, obviously a man of the world, said that the city across the river was the marvel of the land between the rivers, for there was yet another great stream, the Tigris, flowing roughly parallel to the east of the Euphrates. The refugees dared look upon that "sin city," their future home. And what they saw was glorious: shining towers reaching to heaven in bold defiance; a manmade garden planted with trees thrusting high above the clamor of the street, a veritable mountain.

"It was built for one of the great king's wives who was homesick for the mountains of Chaldea. I suppose plenty of Jews toiled on that one, too," explained the young servant who accompanied them.

Jeduthun quailed. He had never before seen any place more glorious than Jerusalem and now he was afraid to face the heathen metropolis with only his voice to carry them through.

"O Lord God, look down in pity on Thy servant, for I am stricken dumb. Regard not my sins; have compassion on my weakness. Remember the former days. Bring back Thy songs of praise to my throat that Thy glory may not be lost in this strange land. Strengthen me for Thy mercy's sake, 0 Lord, our help and our redeemer."

After prayer he felt better and resolved to speak to his host about leaving. But Hanan wanted to talk about the contents of the chest brought so painfully through the long march. Jeduthun named his musical instruments lovingly: psaltery, harp, timbal, cymbals, reeds, and stringed instruments. About the scrolls, he was not sure. They would be ancient and precious from the manner in which the old priest described them. The result was that servants were ordered to bring in the chest.

Then it stood before them. Its cedar wood was polished and shining, its carving showing lighter glints from the deep red. Jeduthun removed the heavy lid and reached within. A cloud of desert dust swirled up and sent him gasping against the wall.

Hanan, alarmed, sent for the doctor and had the singer taken back to his benzoin cubicle. He thought a minute and then summoned an old woman, who had delicate hands and loved music. She was told to remove the contents, clean them and the inside of the chest. "Unroll and wipe the scrolls! Don't leave a particle of dust on anything!"

The woman bowed and smiled her pleasure at such a congenial task. Hanan's mind lingered on the scrolls. He wanted to buy them, but feared that Jeduthun would insist on giving them to him out of gratitude. Hanan could not get the treasures out of his mind, for he appreciated antiquity and beauty both for the pecuniary possibilities as well as for their messages of heritage. He must find the right home for the last of the legacy.

When Jeduthun had recovered and once again visited his benefactor, he found the chest ready for him. He displayed the instruments with pride and crooned to them like a mother to her child, his once mighty voice purling in gentle eddies of sound. The great psalm of jubilation that he had formerly shouted in brilliant bursts was sweet and soothing, a welcome and reminder in a strange land:

> *"Praise ye the Lord. Praise God in His sanctuary: praise Him in the firmament of His power.*
> *Praise Him for His mighty acts: praise Him according to His excellent greatness.*
> *Praise Him with the sound of the trumpet: praise Him with the psaltery and harp.*
> *Praise Him with the timbrel, and dance: praise Him with stringed instruments and organs.*
> *Praise Him with the loud cymbals: praise Him with the high sounding cymbals.*
> *Let everything that hath breath praise the Lord. Praise ye the Lord.* "[10]

From that day forward Jeduthun had more breath, partly due to the doctor's redoubled attention. He made Jeduthun recall and practice his very first singing lessons. "Easy does it." "Don't strain." "No, no, sweet and low." The physician laughingly told his colleagues that he was giving music lessons to the lead singer of the Asaph choir. He also gave him soothing potions and gargles. Jeduthun began to vocalize lightly. In time, he was leaping over intervals and drawing sound from deep within his chest.

Hanan summoned both Jeduthun and his daughter to dine. He had for the moon past been busy with affairs across the river. Factotums were constantly coming and going between the house and the warehouses; the old cripple himself had even been rowed over several times; and every evening he sat long over the accounts. Always in the back of his mind was the desire for a plan to preserve the heritage and make it fruitful. At last he called his guests to him and told them his will:

"Listen, dear friends, and accept the gift that comes to you from a very old man who wishes to leave behind a good deed for the future. I would that my noble son Neziah were here to share in this plan, but he sends word from the East that he is delayed for six months, maybe a year. I cannot wait so long. I know his good heart will concur in such an act to further God's grace."

"Listen carefully and prayerfully, dear friends, for it is into your hands that I leave the fulfillment of the promise."

"In the old city on the east side of the river lives a venerable priest, Eleazar, who was old when we came here together at the beginning of our uprooting. He has a house, a gathering place, for all the Jews who live in that neighborhood. They come together at various times for prayer and a little worship, a harking back to better days in the Temple of Solomon. On the Sabbath, the seventh day of rest when they do no work, they come in, great numbers to follow the prayers and rituals of Eleazar, the priest. They bring offerings, but they are poor, and sometimes they forget the Sabbath for they must of necessity toil with their hands even on the Lord's day."

"In this neighborhood among our countrymen, I give you also a house. A small house, the one we first occupied when we came to Babylonia." Hanan paused and smiled. "It was only later after God had prospered us that my wife and daughter had the notion to move over here. They said this air was better for the children and there would be space for them to run and play."

He resumed his serious tone:

"Your house is an ordinary one in these parts. A walled courtyard separates it from the street. There are rooms on the ground floor for work and reception, and on the floor above for sleeping. I hope you will find the roof strong enough to use in the cool of the evening and I have had a new, street-level floor raised so that the refuse from the outside does not pour in when it rains. So much for the practical details of the house that I give you."

"But hear and remember, O Jeduthun. You carry by God's gift the seeds of the future. You will live in Babylon to plant them among His chosen. God guide you to do His will:"

  Exile

   A week later the little family left their refuge in the house of Hanan and crossed the river into the very core of wickedness, the center of cult and king in the most wicked city since Sodom: Babylon.

---

[10] Psalms 150

Chapter 4
The Settlement

Jeduthun, Lily, and Ethan were ready and waiting when Bunah, Hanan's steward, came to them from the main house. His master sent regrets that he could not accompany his guests to their new home, for he was in much pain, unable to leave his bed. Bunah would be their guide and see that they were settled comfortably. Tamar and Atab would follow with their more personal belongings in a separate boat.

They walked to Hanan's jetty and entered a luxuriously cushioned skiff with four oarsmen. The Judeans became nervous at the sight before them as soon as they cleared the line of date palms that fringed Hanan's compound. The mighty Euphrates stretched north and south as far as the eye could see, and their eyes had never seen so much water. The frail craft that would carry them across appeared most unstable, but they pretended to be unconcerned.

Jeduthun had resolved not to look upon Babylon, the great whore, the sink of iniquity. Bunah, however, spoke enthusiastically of the panorama, and Lily and Ethan were so awe-stricken that the singer raised his eyes and was dazzled.

"Look to the north, Maestro. You see that gorgeous green structure? The Ishtar Gate where their Sacred Way enters the city. You must see it in more detail later. The paving is a piece of work the like of which is not to be found elsewhere.

"Next is the great king's palace. Huge, isn't it? Look over against the back and you'll see the famous hanging gardens. Yes, there are trees on top. They say Nebuchadnezzar built it for his queen, who was homesick for her mountains. There's some sort of fancy system to bring water up from cisterns. Clever, these Babylonians."

Jeduthun, not at all interested in the hydraulic system that watered a manmade mountain, was focusing on the splendor that lay almost directly before them. Its ceramic tiles shone in different colors the full extent of its height—seven stories—each smaller than the one below. There was gold at the top, perhaps a shrine.

"The ziggurat of Babylon," said Bunch.

"The Tower of Babel?" asked Jeduthun.

"Perhaps the confusion of tongues, but the word 'Babel' means gateway of the gods."

"Still presumptuous any way you see it, eh, Ethan?" said Jeduthun dryly and poked his wide-eyed grandson.

"What do you mean 'presumptuous'?" the child asked. And while the elder groped for a simpler word, he supplied his own:

"Presumptuous is pretty. Pretty. I like it."

His mother managed a laugh, but Lily was feeling the full force of Ullah's snub: she was indeed a simple country girl facing the golden cup that Babylon held out.

The boatmen had been skillfully weaving through a stream of barges going south. Suddenly, in mid-river, they turned left and passed under the bridge which tied the old city to its newer half. Then the exiles had their first view of a vast structure, not so high as the others, but even more richly decorated.

"The Temple of Marduk," announced Bunah.

"Who is he?" asked Jeduthun.

'The great god of Babylon, greatest of all the other gods."

"How many others, may I ask?"

"Oh, hundreds, thousands."

"So ridiculous."

"But Marduk is the biggest one you ever saw. And covered with gold. Maybe wood underneath. Maybe clay like everything else. Who knows? They bring him out for New Year and even the king pays homage."

"This is the silliest thing I ever heard of."

"Not as silly as you might think," replied Bunah, proud to display his knowledge. "Those priests are the richest men in this rich city. They own lands and till it with slaves. They buy and sell in the market. They keep funds for safety and lend it at usury. Nebuchadnezzar has given them tons of gold for Marduk and plenty of jewels and fragrant woods. Why, those priests make ours in Jerusalem look like beggars—which they may well be."

Jeduthun and his party could only gasp at such opulence and such effrontery.

They were approaching a jetty which ran into a large warehouse.

"This is the seat of Prince Hanan's business-warehouse, market, counting house, and camel yard. We will go in and disembark and walk to your house on Shoe Street."

This they did. Under the shed they savored the smell of rare herbs; out on the street it was garbage that assaulted the nostrils. They picked their way through rubbish on a narrow, twisting lane that wound around a jumble of walls.

"Houses?" asked Lily.

"Yes, said Bunah. "And here's yours."

He opened a small door and flung it back against thick, windowless walls. They went into a vestibule and kicked off their sandals. It was wonderfully cool, opening into a courtyard protected from the sun by a balcony and awnings supported by poles.

Rachel Stern

"What a delightful and refreshing place. Give Hanan our thanks." Lily had a rush of domesticity and was already rearranging the furniture. Tamar and Atab watched with shining eyes the pleasure they had helped bring to "their" family.

Bunah, the fount of information, continued to explain the arrangement. "You see, there are no windows on the streets. The rooms open onto this courtyard. That's the drain to carry off water when—and if—it rains. The family sleeping rooms are up these stairs. Here below are kitchens and work rooms. Places for storage. See? Now come over here. This handsome room is for the reception of guests. Hanan had many when he lived here. That was ten years ago when we first arrived from Jerusalem. Now, as you know, he has his estate across the river, but he keeps his business in the old place."

Having duly impressed his audience, Bunah next directed their attention to the end of the courtyard opposite the vestibule. "That door leads to the bathroom. Modern comfort. The very latest. But you, of course, would know all about such things."

He gave them a minute to admit that they did not. And then he told them and showed them: "At this end, the bathing facilities. One part the ceramic tub with drain, here basins and ewers. Over there are two stalls, each with a voiding stool. All floors and walls sealed in bitumen!"

He paused long enough for the country folk to express their pleasure at the lack of dust or mud before he continued: "The greatest improvement of all you can't see. When we raised the floor to keep out the overflow from the street, we put in a kitchen drain pipe that washes out the voiding seats. Splendid, isn't it?"

Jeduthun and Lily longed to be left alone in their fine new home, but Bunah stayed for dinner. There was an abundance of food brought over from Hanan's kitchen and so Tamar quickly laid out a precooked meal of fish, salad, fruit, barley bread, and honeyed oat cakes. They washed it down with a mild date wine, Bunah talking all the while. His subject was the greatness of the House of Hanan, its charities, its wealth, the vastness of its enterprises—and its peerless son, Neziah ben Hanan, soon to succeed his father. A worthy son of a worthy father, and on and on ....

The newcomers were nodding when the steward finally took his departure, an action that considerably revived them. Lily discovered that some of the furniture could not be moved: benches of clay built up from the floor and backed by a wall. Cushions, more cushions. Jeduthun found ample shelves for his musical instruments in a ground floor room that he immediately claimed as his private quarters. Atab claimed credit for the shelves. Tamar organized her kitchen. The little boy Ethan "helped" everybody, darting from one to the other, always underfoot and being kissed out of the way.

In the weeks following, as they settled into their routine, that fat cherub became increasingly the center of their attention and a chief source of entertainment. For him, his mother had Natab make a mud box in a corner of the courtyard. Here, the boy built ziggurats and hanging gardens without end. He found little playmates to share in the fun of kicking them down. Lily took the leveling a step further: she had the boys smooth the clay and on it she marked with a stick the Hebrew letter A, aleph. They copied it and felt proud, especially as they learned more letters and could say them and write them like a real scribe.

Ethan was a happy, singing child. He went about humming or chirping his own little ditties about the river (where does it go?), about the tall tower (what's up there?), about camels and donkeys and dogs and cats. One day Jeduthun heard him on the subject of Nebuchadnezzar:

"Nebuchadnezzar is a very bad man ...but not as bad as some..."

It was at this point that the grandfather decided he had better take over the musical education of his grandson—more songs of Zion, less improvisation.

They started with the simple one created by pilgrims to the holy city. And Ethan, who adored his grandfather and was a perfect mimic, was soon strutting and bawling weighty matters with all the seriousness of a choir master. In due course, the family would settle down after the evening meal and have a bit of music. Ethan would say, 'Abbi, will you play my 'companiment'?" And Jeduthun would take up one of his stringed instruments and play an elaborate introduction. Ethan would take his stance, feet wide apart, chest full of air, arms at rest, eyes in contact with the maestro. At the signal, he would raise his arms and release the air in the best baritone he could produce:

> *"Lord, my heart is not haughty, nor mine eyes lofty: neither do I exercise myself in great matters, or in things too high for me.*
> *Surely I have behaved and quieted myself, as a child that is weaned of his mother: my soul is even as a weaned child.*
> *Let Israel hope in the Lord form henceforth and forever more."*[11]

His audience would cry "amen" and ask for more. But when the child attempted profundities they could not suppress their mirth. Tamar would run from the room as Ethan intoned:

> *Out of the depths have I cried to Thee, O Lord...."*[12]

Jeduthun was grateful for his heavy beard, but even he, at times, would have a fit of coughing when he saw in the tyke the very spit and image of a Hazan in full spate. The bond between the two was strengthened day by day. The pair were inseparable. Of course, they loved Lily, too—and Tamar—but they were women, born to make men comfortable; therefore, negligible. They merely talked of food, clothing, and shelter: boring.

Jeduthun's renown spread throughout the Jews in the neighborhood so that he was soon giving music lessons to men and women who brought payment. They, in turn, broadened his social contacts to include the old priest, Eleazar, who had come out in the first wave with Hanan. Hanan had given Eleazar a house, which served the community as a gathering place on the day of rest—the seventh day, or Sabbath, as they were beginning to call it in Babylonian fashion.

The priest and the choir master had many interests in common, going back to the reforms of Josiah. They had long talks together, much concerned with the future of their faith and their people in the heathen land, where ten tribes had already been swallowed up by the materialist, amoral culture. They agreed that the prophets were right and that something had to be done to preserve their heritage. Hanan abundantly supplied both houses with food and other necessities.

The heat of summer wore itself out and gave place to chill and rain. This too, passed and spring once more brought life to earth and a rush of water to the river. Babylon was abuzz with talk of New Year's festivities when all the gods of Mesopotamia would come to honor Marduk and the great king would "take the hand of Bel."

The little Jewish community, itself aloof from such stupidity, was especially delighted when a new face appeared in their midst: Neziah ben Hanan, no less, home from a far-ranging caravan expedition. He came first to the house of Jeduthun accompanied by two servants bearing hampers and jars of delicacies.

"Maestro, I am Neziah, the son of Hanan, who sends you greetings and best wishes."

"Come in, come in. I am honored. Let us sit here." Jeduthun led him into the reception room and called out to Lily to bring refreshments. The two men talked of Hanan's declining health.

Lily almost dropped her tray; she had never before seen such a handsome man, or so much of one. Neziah was different! Instead of the robe down to the ankles, he wore a sort of kilt, knee length, of dazzling white linen instead of the usual dingy earthcolors. A close-clipped beard revealed the lines of his jaw and mouth while his hair was cropped in military fashion. The woman served and was ignored.

Neziah noticed her surprise at his appearance and said, "Yes, I have been on caravan most of my life, and I've learned to adapt myself to the road. Those Achaens whom I hob-nobbed with in Sidon are very practical, and it is from them that I learned the most. Of course, I'd be a scandal here if it were not for my father's high position." Neziah helped himself to more honey cakes and gave his short barking laugh, "Ha!"

He paused for Jeduthun's comment, which was not forthcoming. Then he went on: "No matter. I shall not change to please people who know nothing of getting on and off camels, in and out of boats, that sort of thing. Ha! Besides, I like the style."

Lily wanted to say, "I do, too," but like her hairy, berobed father, remained silent. They turned to less controversial subjects. Neziah took his departure, promising to return.

A month or so later he did return, pleading much business as the reason for not coming sooner. After that Neziah came more often, though at irregular intervals, and his friendship with Jeduthun grew firmer. The two men respected each other and listened with interest to what the other had to say. The bounty of Hanan continued, and Lily served without interrupting.

One day as she leaned forward to fill Neziah's tiny wine cup, he turned abruptly and found his face pressing against a softness, very female. After that he began to look at the daughter of Jeduthun and what he saw delighted him. She was not just a pretty girl, but a very beautiful young woman: with a crown of black braids from which curly tendrils brushed pink ears and a delicious neck; straight brows above deep brown eyes; red lips like rose petals parted slightly over perfect teeth. Or was there a slight irregularity in the two front uppers? Were they waiting to be kissed? And what treasurers lay hidden under her shapeless brown dress? Neziah could only speculate but, as a business man, he was not given to speculation. He must get the facts.

On subsequent visits he stole repeated glances at Lily, the desirable, and decided that she was hungry for love. She desired a man though she did not know it. He would rouse her and satisfy her latent passion. He would kiss that mouth—he would!

---

[11] Psalms 131
[12] Psalms 130

Chapter 5
Lily

Once more, the baking sun gave way to winds and cold weather. Jeduthun and his priest friend, Eleazar, worked at making the gathering place more official and more attractive. Eleazar blew the ram's horn early every seventh day. Jeduthun trained his singers to give the priases of Israel regularly on that day of rest. This was followed by an elder reading from one of the scrolls brought by Eleazar from the Temple. The people would have a meal from their baskets, after which Lily's pupils would recite their letters and someone would tell one of the stories of their forefathers: Abraham, who had come from Ur; Adam, whose garden lay between the rivers; Noah, whose ark came to rest in the northern mountains. Most dear of all the tales was that of Moses leading the people from brick making in Egypt to their home in the promised land.

This story was keenly felt as they saw many of their friends reduced to making brick at a beggarly wage. In this land with no stone and very little wood, the bricks were all about them, the only material for ordinary buildings, formed from mud deposited by the river and baked in the sun. Would not some deliverer lead them back to their homeland, promised to the sons of Jacob? Great prophets promised even more. Fed by hope, the congregation increased in numbers and in fellowship.

Neziah's visits to Jeduthun's house also increased. He even went with them to gatherings at the house of Eleazar. His eyes sought Lily and occasionally their glances met briefly. Yet he could not contrive to find her alone. Surely she must know....

One day he came to the house and caught the family at an awkward moment. They were all standing in the doorway watching Atab and another stout fellow carry away the elegant chest of polished cedar brought from Jerusalem packed with scrolls and musical instruments. Lily fled as soon as she saw him coming. She was crying. Her father welcomed the guest warmly as he always did and told Tamar to bring something cool.

"The lady Lily is perhaps not well?"

"She is sick with selfishness," Jeduthun answered dryly. "She does not want to give the old chest for the Lord's work at the gathering place."

In the course of the ensuing conversation, Neziah learned that the priest felt the need of the container for the scrolls Jeduthun had already donated, and Jeduthun felt the need of a focal point of worship on the west wall, toward Jerusalem. The chest would fill both needs. He urged ben Hanan to come and see it in place next Sabbath. The older man truly enjoyed the younger's company and so they chatted amiably for an hour or so. When Neziah left, however, he did not go back to his warehouse by the river but turned in the direction of the house of Eleazar. Jed watched him go and was glad to find him so interested in matters other than business.

Three days later, Eleazar sent the chest back with a message that he had a better one. Jeduthun's pride had to be swallowed, for shortly after, the old priest himself came with an explanation. It seems that Neziah ben Hanan said that it was not fitting to pile scrolls on top of each other from the top. No, the housing for the scrolls should open from the side so that the precious documents could rest on their wooden handles and be displayed without damage. And, lo, that worthy son of Hanan had provided just such a container, beautifully crafted in ebony. It had two doors opening from the side. Jeduthun must come right away and see.

Lily stayed behind to polish and place her beloved chest. She thought it would be empty, but lying in the bottom was a folded square of the thinnest, smoothest material she had ever handled. Could this be silk—from Cathay? A bit of papyrus fell out. On it was written "For Lily." She tried to hide it, but Tamar, who had a long nose for everyone's business, winked and said, "The old priest didn't send you that."

During this second winter, while the hamis blew desert dust and biting cold kept folk indoors, the two women were much occupied with finishing the weaving of warm garments. Lily began to take an interest in cooking, Tamar acting as teacher. There was not time for daydreaming, she told herself. And the monotony of her work enabled her to do just that; busy her hands while her head was filled with dreams of Neziah ben Hanan.

The musical evenings at home, started by Ethan's solos, attracted other people. Some came to sing, others to listen. They sang secular songs of the threshing, of the vintage, of love, of flowers and trees.

Jeduthun coached them and the singers took on a semblance of organization, meeting once a week in the evening. The regulars brought friends and refreshments. Neziah ben Hanan became a regular. He brought a friend, who engaged Jeduthun to perform at a feast. Other engagements followed so that before the year was out the great hazan was fully employed in his chosen profession.

With the coming of warm weather, Neziah had a suggestion: "When we used to live in this house, we sat on the roof after the sun went down. It was most cool and pleasant."

Tamar had an objection: "The roof would cave in if we all went up there. Besides, we'd have to haul up chairs and everything."

The next day workmen reinforced the rafters and laid a heavy matting of palm thatch. They repaired an old ceramic core which could be lifted and allow the heat from below to escape. Neziah was pleased with his inspection and said firmly, so that Tamar could hear: "Everyone will bring up his own cushion and lean against the parapet."

Neziah's beneficence was boundless. He brought a gorgeous tile game board, the royal game of Ur, he said, for three players. He taught Jeduthun and his daughter the chief moves and was amused to watch Lily carefully refrain from winning. "The girl is quick of mind as well as hand," he chuckled.

One night he came late to the roof and found Lily in a dark corner holding Ethan's sleepy head in her lap. While the others sang a languorous song, Neziah's hand found its way through her sleeve to her breast. He fondled her. She did not respond one way or the other, but when the hand slid down toward her secret parts, she jumped up like a scalded cat and ran, dragging Ethan with her.

Afterward, as he rowed home across the river, Neziah thought, "The woman is a prude. She doesn't know what she is missing. I could...." He looked at his hand, brought it to his mouth. And suddenly, he was engulfed by a wave of protective love. For the first time in his life, he wanted to give without hope of reward, to help without thought of gain.

He pulled his oar more rapidly, setting his boatman a stroke hard to maintain. Then he slowed as he mused, "Perhaps she thinks I am too old for her." Perhaps he was. She was only a few years older than Azez, his first born. He thought of his wife Ullah, that disagreeable and discontented woman. These matters would have to be sorted out. And Lily's husband, who might appear any day—surely he was dead?

As the musicale was breaking up, Neziah had brushed close to Lily and whispered, "I'll come for you in an hour. We must talk."

She did not have time to say "no" before he was gone. An hour later, he scratched at the door and she was ready. He handed her into a covered litter and ran alongside to his warehouse. There he helped her into his person skiff, manned by two oarsmen in the stern. Lily found herself beside him on a cushioned seat protected by an awning, which the owner adjusted to black out his crew. They shoved off.

Their boat slipped into the lines of boats heading north but stopped short of the city wall and pulled to one side. Neziah took Lily's hand and told her that he loved her, that she was the woman of his dreams. Could she not love him? She whispered, "Yes." They talked about the difficulties of their situation. He kissed her desperately. He took her home, promising to come again soon.

"No," she said, "It cannot be."

A week passed. No sign of Neziah. Lily began to worry. Had she been too cold? Another week had her drooping with anxiety. She had lost her love. Then, one bright morning, as Babylon was in a festive mood and motion for the New Year's appearance of Marduk, and the fertility rites at the temple of

Ishtar, a servant came bringing the sad news that Hanan was dead. Jeduthun and his household were invited to the funeral. It would be on the morrow, and a barge would come to the warehouse jetty for them.

Jeduthun smote his head and tore his robe in unfeigned grief. "I shall come as chief mourner and sing the lament for our departed friend."

In the cortege of funeral barges the next day, Lily found herself among the women mourners. She caught a glimpse of Neziah and his family: Neziah, looking stricken and bewildered, his proud wife overly dressed, and their two lively sons properly subdued. She heard her father's magnificent voice intone:

> *"O Hanan, we shall not see thy likes again. Out sorrow follows thee to thy grave."*

She could feel Neziah shudder at the thought of his beloved father buried, but not with his fathers....

"But in a kingdom that calls not upon our God," the great singer went on to praise the deeds of Hanan. "Who fed us within his gates when we came as strangers to this strange land."

Lily and all the people recalled the good works of Hanan who was "chosen by God to be his right hand among the children of Israel..." They wailed and wept. "O God, give ear to our sorrow."

They were rowed beyond the outer wall to the Jewish cemetery. There they lowered their good friend, that good man Hanan, to his final resting place.

> *"O God, forget not Thy servant Hanan. Show us Thy mercy and Thy peace."*

They went home weeping. Lily wanted to reach out and take Neziah into her arms and comfort him. She ached for him in his sorrow.

If she could only let him know.

Chapter 6
Neziah

It was two moons before Neziah again appeared at the evening musicale. Looking tired and haggard, he sat beside Lily. She took his hand and brought it to her breast. The hand found its way under her dress, and she let him fondle her as he would. While the party was breaking up, he pressed against her and whispered, "Will you come with me in the boat soon?" And she nodded.

But it was not to be soon. Neziah had much business and an insatiable wife. She would drag him into bed and, in the darkness, he would pretend that he lay with the lovely young Lily.

"Ah, husband, you have regained your youth,' Ullah would sigh after she had had all that any woman could ask.

"Hah! Perhaps I have," he would mumble, half asleep.

As for Lily, she went about her chores in a dream. The thump of the loom was the stroke of oars; the whir of the spindle the whispering of love. "He is coming. He loves me." It was all that she could think about. No wonder Tamar scolded when she let the fish burn. 'Act your age!" said Tamar, but there was a sympathetic twinkle in her eye. Besides, she liked Neziah and the bits of silver he pressed into her hand.

Opportunities were found, and the lovers did manage to be alone together on the river. Neziah would bring a covered litter for Lily after bedtime, or when Jeduthun was away from home making music The man and woman would enter the boat, be rowed up river for the cool breeze, and hold long conversations about their hopeless situation. All the while they would be kissing and fondling, but Lily always stopped him short of penetration and consummation. They passed almost the whole summer in a sweet agony of repressed desires.

And then one night, the inevitable happened.

When they fell apart, Neziah murmured in her ear, "My love, I did not think to find you such a virgin."

"It has been years since I have known a man."

"Did I please you?"

"My dear Neziah, I never knew that lying with a man could give such pleasures."

"But your husband...?"

"We were young and he was always in a hurry."

"But surely he …."

"No. He was attentive to his husbandly duties, but I was only a receptacle …."

"The boor! We shall have to make up for lost time!"

"Yes, my love."

But on the way home Lily began to weep and tremble. He understood and held her close, as she had a bad case of nerves.

Inside the house she fell into Tamar's arms sobbing, "O, I am so afraid."

"Did you…? Did he…?" Lily had to confess that "we did."

"Never fear," the older woman comforted her. "Here. Drink this." And she handed her a small cup of bitter herbs. Lily drank and made a wry face.

"Here. Eat this." It was a honeyed fig. "You'll see. I am prepared to take care of you. Do not fear. It is the way of all living creatures. Quite natural, you might say. Now get a good night's sleep."

Lily slept fitfully between dreams of sexual satisfaction that were new to her. From her limited experience she felt that Neziah was uniquely fitted to be her mate, therefore her true husband. And in subsequent trysts she shared her belief with him. He was happy to agree: "You are truly my bride. You have brought back my youth."

And so they made love whenever they could. Sometimes there were long months of separation while Neziah went to inspect his entrepots which extended from the lower sea on the east to the upper sea on the west. Sometimes there were periods when they lay together frequently. Always, they gave and received pleasures that climaxed in orgasm. And always they lay in each other's arms in confidence that knew no disappointment.

Tamar always had bitter herbs ready. She saw her nursling glow with an inner light, her lips twisted slightly in a secret smile that said, "I am beloved." Neziah's servants detected in him a softened manner of speaking. Prompted by a rumor, a mere hint from the boatmen, the household of Hanan discovered that the new master had found a woman to love. They were glad, for nobody liked that shrew, his wife Ullah.

One night immediately after the two lovers entered the boat, Neziah said, "My love, are you with child?"

Lily said no.

"Are you sure?"

"Yes, quite sure. Why do you ask?"

Neziah told her that he had to go out with a caravan on a very long journey and did not want to leave her pregnant. He would take her with him if she would go.

Lily wept at the prospect but said that her duties to her father and her son bound her at home. "Some day…."

He held her close but did not enter her that night. Next day he was gone.

Then Lily knew the full force of his love. She thought bitterly of Jarib, the husband who had deliberately left her pregnant to face the toilsome journey to Babylon. She hated him as she remembered that miscarriage which occurred in public and could not be concealed. Neziah would never treat her so. With him she was safe. For the first time she knew protective love: the man would take care of her instead of being taken care of. The feeling so contrasted with her position as daughter, wife, and mother that she felt freedom and relief from a heavy load she had carried all her life. Neziah would keep her safe.

Neziah, for his part, knew for the first time what it meant to care for someone more than himself. Perhaps he had felt something of it for his father, especially in the last days of his illness. But the lover did not recognize any similarity when he thought of that exquisite young woman, wasting her beauty in household drudgery for an old father and a boy, both self-centered and unmindful of her services. He vowed to take her out of that dreary house and into his own.

The old father and the boy were too preoccupied with their own affairs to notice the change in Lily. Jeduthun welcomed Neziah and his gifts, but went steadily about more serious matters—his music. He found that he could compose poems and sing them and teach them to his chorus groups. He was even giving lessons on stringed instruments to certain talented pupils. He and the old priest were often together pouring over the scrolls and selecting passages for the Sabbath reading. They wanted to make sure that the assembly knew the treasurers of their past, the hopes of their future.

The boy Ethan grew like a weed. "He will be as tall as his grandfather," thought Lily proudly. She watched him romp with his peers, cleaned him up, fed him, and sent him off to be schooled by the scribe in residence at Eleazar's house.

As time passed, the love between Neziah and Lily grew into friendship. They shared confidences and problems, as well as their bodies. And each sought to please and comfort the other by listening sympathetically and offering suggestions when asked.

Neziah spoke freely of his pride in his two sons Azez and Teman, as he taught them his own skills: handling a boat, swimming, riding, and loading camels and lesser animals. There was a scribe for book work, but Neziah and the two boys enjoyed together the outdoor exercises equally useful for business. He took them on short journeys into the desert and splashed with them in the Euphrates, the main artery of commerce.

Lily thought wistfully of her own son's limited experiences, confined to a crowded neighborhood in the old city and to old men. The music lessons were ongoing every moment Jeduthun could spare; Ethan's time was spend memorizing endlessly the Songs of Praise, writing them under the watchful scribe, even copying from one of the old priest's scrolls the wisdom from

Solomon. Fortunately Ethan adored his grandfather, admired the priest, and tolerated the scribe. He enjoyed escaping the women by going to the gathering place, Eleazar's house, for school and scuffling with other boys. That was all well and good. Still, Lily wished that Neziah would take her son under his wing, though she dared not say it.

Neziah occasionally mentioned his wife Ullah. He found her very hard to please no matter what he brought her, no matter what he said or did. She was always berating the servants and scolding the family into sullen silence. A discontented and disagreeable woman was the impression Lily had gotten from bits of anecdotes Neziah told from time to time.

The two lovers were becoming so closely attuned that they could almost read each other's mind. So, when the man spoke of his wife, the woman felt his need to know about her husband. For profound shame, she could not speak. Finally she forced herself to tell her story.

It came out in fits and starts, rapid words and long silences, while Neziah held her and ground his teeth. It was such a pitiable little story:

Lily's mother died when Lily was born. Tamar brought her up. Some female relatives had offered to take her, but Jeduthun would keep her, though he spent most of his time at the Temple. She remembered school as the chief pleasure of her childhood. There were widows who made themselves charming to the little girl and brought goodies as they sought to attract Jeduthun. At length, the ladies gave up. Lily was left with Tamar as her guide to whatever was not found in books.

When Lily was thirteen years old, Tamar told Jeduthun his daughter was ready for marriage. The father brushed aside that information, saying there was no hurry. Tamar felt otherwise and consulted a female relative. In due course a marriage broker arrived, a suitable match was agreed on, and gifts were exchanged.

The groom was to be Jarib, fourth son of a rich merchant who sent caravans for trading throughout Palestine and even Egypt. He was reported to be normal in body, very quick of mind. Any girl should be proud to have such a husband for whom to bear sons. Lily looked forward to an early wedding day, for she suspected (from order girls' whispers and giggles) that the marriage bed was full of delight. She and Tamar redoubled their efforts to fill the chest that had been her mother's, the very one that carried scrolls and musical instruments from Jerusalem, to make it again a bridal chest laden with embroidered garments and girdles. To it, Jeduthun had to add a certain amount of silver. Tamar and the broker handled that. It was a firm betrothal.

The great day came. Toward night the groom arrived with a band of roistering friends. They looked at the beautiful bride with approval and carried her and her chest to Jarib's house for a feast. There was to much food, too much wine, too much noise. Lily was hardly aware of Jarib until he picked her up and flung her on a bed. She knew what to expect and was trying to remove her finery when he slammed into her with a fury of a bull. As the pain subsided she heard the men crowded at the door yelling, "What ails you, Jarib? Keep going! Let us in! We want to see!" The groom took proof of his bride's virginity out to his friends. Lily was so shamed and humiliated that she refused to show herself the next day, or the next. Jarib and his family took that to mean that she was enjoying her bridal.

During the two weeks allowed the groom to devote himself exclusively to his wife, Lily discovered one unpleasant surprise after another. Jarib was short and far from handsome, a lusty youth unskilled in the arts of love. This she accepted like the dutiful wife she was expected to be.

Their bedroom, however, was so small and cramped that there was no place to sit except on the bed, jammed against the wall. There was a table with a bowl, pitcher, and waste bucket beneath, and a few pegs for hanging clothes. The much-traveled chest crowded the small space between door and bed. Their privacy was a boarded-off end of a passageway, and the boards did not groove together or reach all the way between floor and ceiling. Too many people lived in that house. Jarib's father might be a rich man, but none of the three older sons had a house of his own, and each of them had a child to account for every year of his marriage. There were dozens of them.

Like mice, they were all over the place. Like cheese, the bridal chamber attracted them. There were little black eyes peering through the cracks and knot holes. Little feet scampered away when Jarib roared at them. He complained to their mothers, who saw no harm. He complained to their fathers, who laughed uproariously. He complained to his own father, and the old man told him to complain to their mothers.

One pitch-dark night, Lily reached out to brace herself for Jarib's onslaught. Her hand touched one of the brats. She screamed. Jarib picked up his curious nephew, beat his bottom thoroughly, and threw him out squalling.

"Want a closer look, do you? Take this!"

At this point in Lily's tale, Neziah guffawed.

"It wasn't funny," she snapped.

"No, dearest, interrupting coition is never funny. Let me take you home with me where it will not happen to us."

There ensued the familiar propositions and objections that had been going on for years. He would, and she could, if she would. She would not be a second wife, certainly not a concubine. Her father and her son needed her.

It was months later when Neziah learned how Suzannah happened to be living in her father's house instead of her husband's during the siege of Jerusalem.

It seems that Jarib's father found a couple of his grandchildren lying together on the floor of his reception room. They were so intent on the problem of getting his tiny thing into hers that they did not see the old man.

"What do you think you are doing?" he roared.

Exile

"Playing grown up," the girl said pertly.

After that Jarib and his father agreed that maybe it would be better for the young couple to live with her father in a largely empty house. Jeduthun was agreeable.

So, back came the chest, along with Jarib's gear. Jeduthun enjoyed his son-in-law's news of the political situation and the marts of trade. They would converse until Jarib pulled his sleepy wife off to bed with some coarse remark about how she needed his comfort.

It was in such submission that Ethan was conceived. Soon, Jarib had to go north with a caravan, to Lily's great relief.

One evening Neziah spoke of his family's emigration to Babylon in the first punishment visited upon the partisans of King Jehoikim. Nebuchadnezzar's soldiers had carried off the Temple vessels of gold and silver. Hanan carried his portable wealth on camels. "It was shameful but he made it. You were just a little girl then, and I a grown man."

"I remember," replied Lily. "We were glad that we did not have to go. My father's duties in the Temple increased. He was too important there to have time for us at home."

"Do you mean to tell me that the great Jeduthun did not know what was going on?"

"When Jarib came to live at our house, he and Jeduthun talked about it all the time. I'm afraid I didn't listen very carefully but I do know that they talked about a man named Jeremiah who wanted peace with Babylon lest Judea be destroyed. Jarib thought he was an agent of Nebuchadnezzar: Jarib sided with King Jehoikim and trusted Egypt."

"So where was that man of no understanding, that oaf Jarib, when Nebuchadnezzar came down on you the second time?"

"He was on caravan. Still, he slipped through the lines of the besieging army and would have taken us out with him, but my father was determined to wait. He said he would trust the almighty hand of God and rely on the outstretched arm of His deliverance. He made a song about it ...."

"Ezekiel was optimistic, too, I hear. He came out with you?"

"It was very confusing."

"Well, no doubt now. We know Jehoikim was a fool. There's nobody left in Judea except riff-raff to tend the fields and flocks. It's as bad as what Senaccharib did to the northern kingdom a hundred years ago."

"What did happen to the ten tribes?"

"They are scattered all over. Every now and then you run across one who knows he is a Jew, but mostly they are just like Babylonians, as we, too, shall be in the fullness of time."

"Oh, don't say that to Jeduthun."

"Don't worry. I know how to talk to him. So your husband went down into Egypt and hasn't been heard from in all these years?"

"Neziah, you know I fear he will come any day ...."

Neziah, under his breath, cursed that unfeeling oaf and resolved that he should never return. He sent for Amok, a confidential agent who had much experience in handling delicate matters and keeping his mouth shut.

Lily never told her lover about the ultimate indignity of her roadside miscarriage, nor did she tell him about Tamar's bitter herbs. A woman must have some secrets.

Chapter 7
Jeduthun

Jeduthun appeared to be happily busy with his music. When he was missing from his household circle, they assumed he was occupied with his pupils, his instruments, or his composition. Much of the time, however, he spent on his knees, face down toward Jerusalem, in earnest prayer.

Only Eleazar, from long experience as a confessor, felt that his friend was a truly troubled man. The remedy would be wisdom, the wisdom of the old writings on the scrolls he had brought from the Temple. And so the priest engaged the singer in a study of the ancients, ostensibly with a view to selection and comment at the Sabbath assemblies.

Jeduthun was fascinated to discover that his questions and his experiences were not new, not original to him, but shared through the centuries by intelligent, God-fearing men. He poured over Job, the good man who suffered while evil-doers prospered. He identified with Solomon, who had pat advice for every need in Proverbs, but who at the end was the preacher about vanity in Ecclesiastes.

Why? How long? Why am I here? Where am I going? What do you, Lord, want me to do? Jeduthun asked humbly, faithfully, but no answers came.

One day as he stood before his group of singers, ready to rehearse their Sabbath Psalm, he had a strange, out-of-body moment when he seemed to be lifted, moved, and then put back in place. He found himself intoning a history that was a parable. God has spoken: "Teach the children." He was doing just that, and his pupils were fascinated to learn the record of the sons of Jacob coming out of Egypt under the leadership of Moses.

> "...I will utter dark sayings of old: Which we have heard and known, and our fathers have told us.
>
> We will not hide them from their children, showing to the generation to come the praises of the Lord, and His strength, and His wonderful works that He hath done...
>
> That the generation to come might know them...
>
> That they might set their hope in God and not forget the works of God, but keep his commandments . . . . "[13]

Jeduthun could feel his listeners responding with their hearts and desiring to hear more. He did not hesitate to lengthen his song and to give more history in other long songs. Eleazar was enthusiastic, too. He would have the scribe teach history to the school children. Memorize. Memorize.

For a while Jeduthun knew he was doing God's will. He knew why he was here, and now in Babylon with the exiled sons of Judah and Benjamin. He knew where they were going: home to the Promised Land. There was a prophet Ezekiel, saying the same thing. He was up north in the Chebur, in another Jewish enclave, but his words of hope spread abroad whenever the chosen people were settled. Jeduthun felt in tune with something greater than himself.

But was he? His best singers were melting away. His songs lacked ...what?

When his most promising pupil dropped out of sight, Jeduthun made inquiry of his parents. Their son had found work down river digging in Nebuchadnezzar's canal that joined the two rivers to the Lower Sea. Another young man was slave to a priest of Marduk. His father had borrowed money of the avaricious priest and given his son as pledge of payment. Unable to repay the debt, the father had to watch his son taken into slavery.

Other members of the congregation came and seemed to enjoy the Sabbath singing and fellowship, but their attendance was ragged: here one week, missing the next, for one excuse or another, too tired, had to make a journey, sick, or tending the sick. Jeduthun felt himself out of touch, in need of the human support he had sorely missed since the passing of Hanan.

He turned to his immediate family. There was Lily wearing that little, secret smile. Could she be expecting her stupid, loquacious husband?

"Guess he found in bed something better to do than talk," he thought. Aloud he said, "Susi, have you had any word from Jarib lately?"

The smile vanished as she answered, "No, Father, not these five years have we had news of my husband."

"Well, Atab, get you to all the market places and make diligent search for Jarib, who went down into Egypt. He should be here any day now."

Lily turned away lest he see her panic. What would she do if Jarib should appear? What could she do now that she lay in the arms of her true mate? That night their love was especially ardent, for both the man and the woman admitted that they shared the same fear.

His grandson, Jeduthun realized, was growing up and less interested in lessons, especially solo singing. Immediately after meals, he would dash quickly from the house lest he be caught and made to project his voice just so. He was bored with those stale Temple songs. His grandfather might be famous, but he surely was hopelessly old fashioned. Jeduthun missed the old companionship; he sensed the chasm that lay between man and boy. So he contented himself by saying, from time to time, "You are growing like a weed, Ethan." But in the end it was the boy who asked the questions that brought the man back to life.

Jeduthun did what he could for himself by recalling the years of the favor of the Lord. The happy times when he had the memory of every word and every note, when he found the true pitch for his voice, when he learned avidly from all who would teach. The exciting times when he would go to the outer wall, take a deep breath and project his voice over the whole valley and then rein it in like a kite. The challenging times when he gave wings to sound; like a hawk, he would soar and plummet. Like and eagle he would hover at any height and hold. Like a mountain stream, he could roar a great wall of sound or purl in limpid tones. Yes, the years of his youth had been great years of the Lord's favor, of accepting His gift. He had been the wonder of the Asaph choir, of all the Temple musicians.

Jeduthun remembered how his choir had cared for him as if he had been their own child. His father had been one of them, but had gone on a journey and had never again been heard of. They told him later that his mother, whose people had come from Ephraim and Solomon's kingdoms, had agreed desire to see her ancestral home. So, though the times were dangerous with robbers and deserting soldiers roaming at large, the couple, with two older children, had gone north with an armed caravan as far as Gilgal. There they parted and turned west, never to be seen again. The choir gave Jeduthun his father's share of the offerings and all the encouragement he needed to become the chief musician.

One day as he stood in his rank to sing the evening worship, his eyes met those of a girl who was drawing him to her by sheer will. She wore a yellow head scarf and stood in the court of women just below the steps of the choir. Her merry eyes insisted, "Follow me!" Once free of his duties, Jeduthun quickly found her. She darted away at such speed that he could not keep up through the crowd of people in the narrow, twisting streets. She did not wish to be caught, but at every abrupt turn she waited until he saw which way the yellow scarf was going. Finally she dove through the doorway to a small cubicle, a gatekeeper's lodge, and there she welcomed him with open arms and taught him the art of love.

They repeated their game for almost a week until, one evening, the girl said, "Lover boy, this is the last time for us. Tomorrow, I am to be married."

Jeduthun was stunned. "But your husband…"

"He is rich, old, and impotent. He'll be so delighted with me in bed that he'll ask no questions. And he'll be so proud of the son born exactly on time that he'll claim him as his own seed."

They parted without much regret, for each had more important affairs to pursue. Jeduthun was rising rapidly as the star of Temple music—more solos, more choir rehearsals for every feast day. He was even commissioned to compose and sing a special selection for the Feast of Tabernacles. So busy was he for two years that he did not even think of the girl in the yellow scarf.

Then again he saw her and again she led him to the same cubicle for the same purpose. Jeduthun was willing but curious: "Your husband? The child?"

Later she said, "Your voice has grown and your organs, too. Let's do it again."

While she massaged his groin, she whispered in his ear the funny story of the flabby old man who thought he had produced a fine son on his first bridal night.

"The trouble is," she continued, "the silly cuckold wants another. He is driving me crazy with his heavy breathing and grinding into me. I'm worn out with him. You can satisfy him and me, too. Now?"

They had a few nights together and then she quit him. Jeduthun never knew her name or what had happened to her and his children. He completely forgot the whole affair in the happiness of music and marriage.

His older choir members, always faithful to take care of their own, found him a bride. Just before his twentieth birthday, Jeduthun received the slender, delicate Mahalia (a lily) into his home. They had great joy in their lovemaking, but she died of it and left him the girl child whom he named Lily. Mahalia, who did not like her name, had once said she wished she had been named Lily instead. He kept the baby as a reminder of a penalty. Tamar, who had come into the house as Mahalia's servant, brought up the child as best she knew how.

Jeduthun closed the door firmly on painful memories—the protracted torture of Mahalia's giving birth, the agonizing numbness at the loss of the beloved. Was such the favor of the Lord?

On the other hand, he had participated in a great era in the Temple. As a school boy and chorister, he had worked at serving that memorable Passover of good King Josiah. Thousands of oxen and smaller cattle had been slaughtered and cooked and shared out, so many that every priest and Levite toiled all day long that the Holy One of Israel should be duly honored for their deliverance from bondage in Egypt.

King Josiah had dug up, pounded to powder, and burned all pagan altars not only in Judah, but far up into lost Jewish lands. He had cleaned and restored the Temple while the child Jeduthun and his friends jumped about the stones and timbers. The awesome reading of The Book brought home, even to the young, the seriousness of Josiah's effort to bring the people back to the worship of One God. They had gone whoring after strange gods, many gods, ever since King Solomon's day. They were unfaithful to their vows, their covenant relationship sworn to under Moses and Joshua. The Book, an old scroll found in the cleaning of the Temple, was a second giving of the law by Moses. When the people heard it read aloud by the high priest Hilkiah, they understood the enormity of their sin. With them, the young Jeduthun rent his clothes and wept.

There followed such zeal for worship as had not been seen since the time of David and the early days of Solomon. Abundant blood sacrifices filled the

Exile

air with the odors pleasing to Yahweh. Incense ascended to His nostrils. Songs of praise from great choirs honored without ceasing His power and His glory. These were years of the favor of the Lord. Then why did good King Josiah, who did that which was pleasing in God's sight, have to die? And irony of ironies, at Megiddo in battle with Pharaoh Necho?

At least he was spared the wrath and desolation that fell upon Jerusalem ten years later, as the prophetess Huldah had foreseen. Jeduthun mused upon this and the warning of Jeremiah. These were political matters of the court, which he did not even try to follow, and a power struggle between great forces. Judah always seemed to be on the losing side. That much he knew.

Through it all, he sang the high poetry of Israel until he had to face the grim reality of Nebuchadnezzar and the second expulsion to Babylonia. Could this be justice? Why should God's people suffer while those who worshipped abominations triumphed and flourished? And he, the great hazan who had received God's great gift, cultivated it, controlled it, and used it only in God's service. What was he, the chief musician of the Temple, doing with that hit-and-miss collection of fun-seekers in Babylon?

It was all very well for Eleazar to accept the excuses of the defecting Jews. Eleazar advised Jeduthun to do the best he could with what he had and trust in the Lord for the results. But for Jeduthun, the question was: What does the Lord require of me now? He felt an awful silence, detachment, disembodiment. He was shattered, barely held together, the walking dead, a shade. He had to reach out for human support.

Nearest to hand was Ethan, growing like a weed and chattering like a magpie. Evidently those long legs had carried him forth into places where he had no business.

"Marduk is taller than this house. His head is gold. Maybe his feet, too, but he wears shoes full of jewels. His clothes have the most colors you ever—Grandfather, why don't we have a god like Marduk instead of old, mean Yahweh?"

"For shame! You don't know what you're talking about!"

Jeduthun felt the echo inside his skull: "...don't know what you are talking about."

Again he went to the old priest with his problem. Eleazar knew much about Yahweh, very little about people. He was unable to identify with Jeduthun and dared not trust to him such knowledge as he had. The priest saw in Jeduthun a man valuable to the synagogue as a singer but also a threat if he started talking about pagan gods. Who knew how far the unsettling would go?

"Leave it alone," was the substance of what he advised. And Jeduthun was confirmed in his feeling that the priest was long on brains, but lacking in heart.

There was Hanan's son, a sensible fellow in spite of his odd appearance. He would know about the gods of Babylon, for he was a worldly Jew. Neziah came occasionally to Jeduthun's house bringing gifts. Yes, he honored his father and his father would be proud of him, but he did not linger in long conversation. In fact, Jeduthun did not see much of him. One night he thought he saw Neziah running alongside a closed litter. But only once. Jeduthun resolved to detain him at the next opportunity and quiz him about the gods of this den of iniquity.

Neziah, for his part, was hard to pin down, and when caught, he seemed uneasy and anxious to be off. When the encounter could no longer be avoided, he followed Lily's father into his private music room and braced himself.

"Den of iniquity?" Neziah echoed in relief. "Just like everywhere else. Just more of it because this is the largest city in the world. As for its gods, I'm as big a dunce about them as I am about music. Interested, but on the fringes."

Under Jeduthun's gentle probing, Neziah told him what he had been able to observe: "Strictly from the businessman's point of view, you understand."

"I guess I don't understand anything you say," replied Jeduthun.

"What has business got to do with God? Yes, the priests of Marduk are rich. They even charge usury. They are sharp lenders. When they lend, if the borrower can't cover his debt, they demand security for repayment, preferably land. Otherwise, the borrower pledges himself or a son to become a slave to the lender, and the heathen priests have no mercy in collecting. No wonder they made Marduk with a golden head."

"Yes, I've heard about the golden calf that was so upsetting to Moses. But then these Priests want to know what Marduk has to say. They look for omens in the entrails of beasts, or the flight or birds, or the curling smoke. How can such accidents have meaning for men? Or give guidance for conduct that pleases God?"

Jeduthun was deeply troubled that this image, made with human hands—and others as bad or worse—should seem to be winning over the God of Abraham, Isaac, and Jacob.

Neziah reflected and then slowly said, "I don't understand it either. The Babylonians are like us and yet so different from us in many ways. They admire success, and Marduk is a winner. He was their city god, and now their city rules the world. So, he is top god. There are many others ...."

"Yes, like that female at the other end of Procession Street—Ishtar—whose gate opens into this city."

"That's the same as Ashtereth. We had her fertility idols all over our country."

"The good king Josiah cleaned them out. And yet Yahweh destroyed him...." Jeduthun began to pace about the room, assailed by guilty thoughts of the girl in the yellow scarf.

Neziah looked down at his hands and found them clenched. He silently cursed himself for a ninny that he did not come right out and claim the older man's daughter as his wife.

Jeduthun broke the silence: "It is hard to explain to a boy the nature of Yahweh, but I cannot have him going to those temple harlots that are underfoot whenever you turn."

Neziah sighed. "Early marriage is the answer to that one."

Jeduthun's prayers became more fervent. He pleaded with the Most High to make His will known so that he could truly serve Him. There was only silence.

One Sabbath Jeduthun stood before his little choir to conduct the early worship music. There were few in the congregation. All looked toward the east at the sun emerging from a pink haze. The hazan lifted his hand and his voice, and they began:

"The heavens declare the glory of God, and the firmament showeth His handiwork."

Day unto day uttereth speech, and night unto night showeth knowledge—"[14]

The magnificent voice continued into solo. Jeduthun had left his choir and his earthly stance. He was transported.

"There is no speech nor language, where their voice is not heard.

Their line is gone out through all the earth, and their words to the end of the world. In them He hath set a tabernacle for the sun,

Which is like a bridegroom coming out of his chamber, and rejoiceth like a strong man to run a race.

His going forth is from the end of the heaven, and his circuit unto the ends of it; and there is nothing hidden from the heat thereof.

The law of the Lord is perfect, converting the soul: the testimony of the Lord is sure, making wise the simple.

The statues of the Lord are right, rejoicing the heart: the commandment of the Lord is pure, enlightening the eyes.

The fear of the Lord is clean, enduring forever: the ordinances of the Lord are true and righteous altogether.

More to be desired are they than gold, yea, than much fine gold: sweeter also than honey and the honeycomb.

Moreover, by them is Thy servant warned: and in keeping them there is great reward.

Who can understand his errors? Cleanse thou me from secret faults.

Keep back Thy servant also from presumptuous sins; let them not have dominion over me: then shall I be upright, and I shall be innocent from the great transgression.

Rachel Stern

> *Let the words of my mouth, and the meditation of my heart, be acceptable in Thy sight, O Lord, my strength and my redeemer.*"[15]

Jeduthun's face shone from an inner light. He sat down. He did not know at what point he had detached himself from his choir. He did know that his God had spoken to him and through him. And he knew that his response had been accepted.

---

[13] Psalms 78
[14] Psalms 19
[15] Psalms 19

Chapter 8
By the Rivers of Babylon

Jeduthun's song caused a mild stir on the day it was sung. Ethan, who had stood with the women on their side of the choir, was most enthusiastic. Walking home alongside his grandfather, he said, "Abbi, you really took off today. It was beautiful! We were with you to put praise into the sky, but then you left us and started to come down, slowly, in a circle, like a big bird."

Jeduthun looked down into the shining face and responded, "I'm glad you liked it."

"Oh yes, it was beautiful, especially at the end when you came down so low in prayer."

Ethan put his hand on his stomach. "I wish I could get music from down there."

"You will. You will. Give it a few more years and don't strain on those high tones."

"I bet I can sing your new song right now."

"Save your breath until we get home. Better yet, you can write it down for me." Jeduthun could not recall much of his new composition, but he knew Ethan had inherited a phenomenal musical memory. He hugged his mystical experience to himself lest it slip away, or worse, lest he be guilty of presumption. Who would understand?

Lily, who had arrived late at Eleazar's gathering place, reported the audience's admiration. Tamar, who had arrived later still, said, "I told 'em they ought to have heard you in the Temple. These oafs can't appreciate real music." And Atab, who didn't come at all, made himself small in a corner.

So Ethan set himself the task of writing out the words of the psalm. He would sing a phrase, make an up or down line, indicating voice direction and underneath put the words. It was fun, especially when his grandfather looked over his shoulder and smiled approvingly. But it took time, and Ethan didn't have much time.

He had been apprenticed to a shoemaker, who worked him all morning. The afternoons were spent at school. By the time he had reached home, he was so tired he could manage only a few lines of the intricate letters that adorned the precious scroll Jeduthun had lent him. He took it to school, where the scribe encouraged him to spare no pains for perfection.

"You must understand the message, my boy. Your lesson for tomorrow will be to explain the general meaning of the song and then, explain line by line."

Ethan balked. "'Aw, no fair. You sing music, you don't explain it." His teacher was firm, however, and so the boy took his problem to the old priest. Eleazar said he had more important things to do than to answer silly questions. That left Jeduthun, the source of the trouble.

"Ethan, my son, that hymn came to me by inspiration, I can't explain it fully. But God seems to be saying that he reveals himself to us on two levels: the natural law and the moral law, given to Moses. See how great is Yahweh. His moral law is greater than Marduk.

"Law?"

"Rules."

"I hate rules. I just can't stand all this stuff. The teacher says you've got to do everything his way." Ethan pursed his lips and gave a good imitation of the scribe. His grandfather suppressed a smile.

"And that bullying old shoemaker. I hate him. Do this. Don't do that. All the time fussing at me—"

Jeduthun was no longer amused. Mind your tongue and respect your elders."

From that day, Ethan was in full revolt. His mother and his grandfather knew the boy was too much for them. They looked at each other in dismay and shrugged their shoulders.

Lily took her problem to Neziah at their trystings. He listened absently, for he was busy with his own desires.

"My love, I do have a plan. Just give me time to straighten out my own affairs and I'll take you home with me, you and your boy, too. And the old man, if he'll come."

She snuggled closer and said, "Some day. Some day." And he proceeded to comfort her in the way they both enjoyed.

Neziah's plan was directed toward the future and it involved moving one piece at a time. First, he had to get his eldest son married, a matter of considerable negotiation with a broker, he explained to Lily when he was finally able to take her into his boat again.

"She's a good match for Azaz. Knows the Babylonian letters and numbers and has a good head for business. I'll establish them in Elam, where they can trade with the silk route merchants before they get here."

It took time, more than Neziah expected. But Lily was used to waiting for him and had her hands full with Ethan and her father besides. The lovers made the most of the precious hours they had together.

The next long delay involved getting Neziah's second son married and established at Damascus. In both cases, Neziah took the bridal couple—and a midwife—to their new abode and stayed with them long enough to see them firmly established.

Exile

"Two years or longer, I guess," he said taking Lily into his arms and entering her." Now all I have to do is put away Ullah, that old bag."

"You are as young and even lovelier than when I first discovered you," he said after they had loved each other. "You are a startlingly beautiful woman, you know."

"How can you tell? We're always in the dark!"

"I don't need light to feel these beauties." There was no mistaking what he meant." And the sweetest are the deepest hidden ...."

Lily's hands stayed busy with domestic chores but her mind had its ups and downs, alternating between dreams of bliss with Neziah and horrors of Jarib's return.

One morning she took her needlework out on the upper balcony to get a stronger light. She heard Tamar and Atab talking in loud whispers which piqued her.

"You said what?"

"I told you, I said I didn't know."

"Didn't know what?"

"Where the chief musician lives."

"Why did he ask you, anyhow?"

"Somebody pointed me out and said I worked for you."

"That's a joke, you lazy dunce. Did the man say what he wanted of Jeduthun?"

"He said it was a family matter."

Lily's heart sank. She ran inside and flung herself on her bed. "I'll not have him again," she sobbed to herself. "I'll throw myself in the river." That would be preferable to the ultimate horror, the law of Moses: death by stoning. If she were taken in adultery with Neziah, the righteous sons of Jacob would drag her out into a field and pelt her with broken bricks until she fell, a bloody pulp, no beauty left for Neziah. That he would be spared was small consolation. "I'll run away!"

She brought her fears to her lover. "You must not worry about that, my dearest. You are a widow and soon you will be my true wife in my home. Long ago, I sent an agent into Egypt. No word has come back. Jarib must be presumed dead after all these years. Come home with me now."

But Lily would not. Her father and her son needed her. Her worst fears, however, were allayed a few days later when Jeduthun came back from Eleazar's house with good news. A scribe had come down from the Jewish settlement on the Chebar, seeking the names of all exiles, their children, and their forefathers. There would be a chronicle so that when they returned to Judea—yes, returned—they could claim the land.

"There is a great prophet at Chebar—Ezekiel—who says that Yahweh speaks to him in visions of new life for us in the homeland."

Lily tried to share this hope but her real interest was in family matters. The names were sought by a chronicler, not a spy for her husband.

Jeduthun saw her smile and continued, "Maybe that's too much for us to hope. Maybe the message is for Ethan's generation or his children. I think I'll go up river right away and see what's going on."

"Father, I think we should find a bride for Ethan before you go."

"Pshaw. Plenty of time for that. No hurry. He's just a kid. Plenty of time for that."

The next day, he boarded a goods barge headed for Mari, leaving Lily with lovesick Ethan on her hands. She was sure it was that cute little girl in the women's choir, who could sing like an angel and was showing all the signs of puberty.

It was while Jeduthun was with his countrymen on the Chebar that they felt the final blow: Nebuchadnezzar drove the last stiff-necked Jews out of Jerusalem and tore down its walls. He pulled apart the very stones of the Temple and left it flat.

Word came from eyewitnesses, treading the long journey to Babylon. Again the conquering king. Again a treacherous ally. Despair rent the people among whom hope, kindled by Ezekiel, had begun to spring. A black despair settled over them. Jeduthun went into a personal and national hell a of doubt, utter discouragement and hatred!

He gave voice to it:

> "By the rivers of Babylon, there we sat down, yea, we wept, when we remembered Zion.
>
> We hanged our harps upon the willows in the midst thereof.
>
> For there they that carried us away captive required of us a song; and they that wasted us required of us mirth, saying, Sing us one of the songs of Zion.
>
> How shall we sing the Lord's song in a strange land?
>
> If 1 forget thee, O Jerusalem, let my right hand forget her cunning.
>
> If 1 do not remember thee, let my tongue cleave to the roof of my mouth; if 1 prefer not Jerusalem above my chief joy.
>
> Remember, O Lord, the children of Edom in the day of Jerusalem; who said, Rase it, rase it, even to the foundations thereof.
>
> O daughter Babylon, who are to be destroyed; happy shall they be, that rewardeth thee as thou has served us.
>
> Happy shall he be, that taketh and dasheth thy little ones against the stones."[16]

Jeduthun returned to his house in Babylon drained, a hollow man. He sat saying nothing, doing nothing, his chin on his chest. Lily was beside herself with anxiety. She prepared delicacies to tempt his appetite. He would taste and say, "Very nice, thank you," and then leave the food on the plate. It was the same with Tamar's more robust dishes of fish or lamb. Ethan, too, did his best to rouse his grandfather from his lethargy. It was hard for him to tone down his youthful exuberance to a level tolerable to the old man. And the boy suddenly saw with pity that Jeduthun was an old man. There was something repellent about being old. Jeduthun was shrinking in body and mind. He was not interested in games or songs or anything; he was completely drawn within himself.

Jeduthun was not thinking of himself, however. He was remembering Zion, once the glory of Israel, wearing a crown of towers and battlements, now a ruin. Once the habitation of the Most High, now a heap of wolves. There was something ghastly about the wreck of a city, worse than rural wasteland. Once people had lived there in their tangled relationships of kinship and fellowship; together they had laughed and cried and prayed and loved and fought and bought and sold and done good and evil. Now they were gone, lost. And the city was a desolation, poles of broken stone. O Jerusalem, how thou art fallen! Why am I left to mourn thee?

Ethan tried his best to make his grandfather go out and see the sights and sounds of Babylon, but he would not. Lily thought going to see his friend Eleazar would do him good.

"I cannot tell him about Jerusalem."

"You don't have to, Father, he knows. And he is sick and he wants to see you very much."

So Jeduthun went to the priest's house, where he found him on a bed of pain in the clutches of a wasting disease. The yellowed skin was drawn tight over the bones as if the winds of time had blasted away all flesh. The priest's eyes lit up when he saw his old friend. Then the lids closed wearily. The two men did not have anything to say to each other, for they breathed as one in sorrow. They longed for the end.

---

[16] Psalms 137

Chapter 9
Ethan

"Father, wake up. This is important. You must attend to this."

"Oh yes, of course. Ethan's marriage. Send the broker in:"

It was driving Lily crazy. Torn between the wasted old man and the lusty youth, she poured out her woes to Neziah, who was running out of patience and sympathy.

"Lily, my dearest, I've turned out Ullah; I have built for you a handsome group of rooms next to mine; I've hired a woman skilled in herbs and unguents for your maid; I've brought a seamstress and handed her the silks that have come from Cathay. My house and my arms ache for you. Come!"

"Neziah, you know I cannot leave my father and my son in their great need of me."

"They will settle down into their own concerns and forget you completely."

"They hardly know I'm there now. But I guess I feel better for doing all I can."

Ethan's marriage was still in negotiations when Tamar tried to persuade him that he could do better.

"What does a big, fine, strapping fellow like you want with a tiny little girl? She's so small you won't be able to find her in bed." Tamar sniggered and Atab guffawed.

Ethan glared. "She's beautiful and she can sing like a bird and I love her!"

"She's a nobody. Who ever heard of her family in Judea? Her father keeps accounts at Hanan's markethouse. He's named Likhi—whoever heard of such a name? He's marrying his daughter 'up', that's what he's doing and he won't even giver her a decent dowry!"

"We don't need money. I'll soon be a master shoemaker, and I'll provide for our needs."

"That will be the day! You better get smart and get yourself a rich wife and quit all this foolishness about 'I love her'." Tamar mimicked Ethan's voice and stricken facial expressions. There were more guffaws and glares.

Ethan was taking himself very seriously at this time, trying to show that he could handle the responsibilities of manhood and head of household.

He toiled at his shoemaker's bench; he was faithful at choir attendance, often taking on the directorship in the absence of his grandfather. He was good at it, for his memory and his ear were accurate. His love of music was so moving that it caught up lesser singers and brought out hidden talent. Singing was a joy for all of them.

Especially Naarah, the small girl with a glorious voice. She could soar to the highest notes and settle down lightly, firmly. No reaching and going just a tiny bit flat. No having to pull her hair to get to the top. Naarah just opened her mouth and waves of music poured forth. And she looked as lovely as she sang. Ethan was captivated. Her eyes rested on him for more than tempo and tune. Their eyes met. They were in love, first love, eager to make sweet music together for the rest of their lives.

Jeduthun was too grieved by the wasting of his friend Eleazar to share his grandson's enthusiasm for marriage. The outrage of senescence was approaching the final indignity—death. Jeduthun was helpless before the sight of a once vigorous and productive man in decay, just lying there. To this end were we created? Jeduthun went to see the sick man, not as often as he should have, to hold his hand and croon softly some of tile grand old praises of Israel.

When Eleazar at last turned his face to the wall and was gathered to his fathers, Jeduthun would not go to the funeral. He could not bear the sight of burial in alien soil; he was haunted by visions of the skeletal body in grave clothes; he felt the chill of approaching union with all the dead who had ever lived. In dirt, decayed. In mud, lost. Into the pit, forgotten.

Ethan and Naarah, full of youth in mind and body, could not possibly share the old man's loss. Their marriage plans moved along.

Ethan perfected his skill as a shoemaker, and by way of proof, brought home his masterpiece, a pair of charming little slippers. These were of red leather sewn with green thread and laced with yellow thongs across the instep. The thongs ended in red balls after passing through green loops attached to the toe and heel pieces. They rested in a small basket of green palm strips, made by the cobbler's wife (who doted upon Ethan and found for him most of the materials that he used).

Lily cried, "Ethan, your slippers are beautiful! They look like bird eggs in their nest. Lovely! They dance! But so small!"

"They are for Naarah," said the boy proudly.

His mother bit her lip to keep from saying that she hoped he would sell them at the market to help toward defraying the wedding expenses.

And at the next choir practice, everyone saw beneath Naarah's plain tunic and straight back, little feet firmly planted in the happiest shoes ever worn by a Jewish maiden.

Tamar remembered a jar in which Jeduthun had tossed bits of silver earned at singing engagements and then promptly forgotten. The bargain was struck and the day set. There was much cooking and embroidering of tunics and girdles. Neziah sent baskets and jars of fruits and fowls.

"He honors his father," said Jeduthun.

"My father, you must speak with Ethan about marriage. He must not go to his bridal bed in ignorance."

Jeduthun smiled for the first time in a year. "The good Lord takes care of such matters. You don't have to give instructions."

But Lily, aware of her painful nuptials, wanted the best for Naarah. She drew Ethan into her room one evening and spoke seriously.

"Ethan, I want to talk to you about marriage. Sit down."

"Aw, Ima, don't. I know all about that. I'm no baby."

She held him firmly with her hands and her eyes and told him that he must go slowly and make sure that his bride was pleased. Ethan flushed scarlet but his mother spared him not.

"It is not enough that Naarah lets you uncover her and enter her. That's her duty. For a happy marriage the wife must have pleasure as well as the husband."

Ethan squirmed and groaned, "Aw, Ima."

"You listen to me. Women are not so easily aroused as men. You must work up her desire for you by fondling and love play. You must control your seed until she is ready. Yes, your wedding night and every other time you lie upon your wife. She must have pleasure every time. That will make for a happy marriage. Take it slowly."

Ethan couldn't decide whether he was going to die of shame or whether he couldn't wait for the great experience with Naarah.

The longed-for day came. The little bride in all her finery was brought from her father's house by the tall, handsome groom and his friends. There was great feasting and drinking, high merriment and much noise. Suddenly there was a hush and a rush. Ethan had picked up his bride and carried her to his room. He slammed the door and bolted it against his uproarious friends, but their cries came through.

"Let us in!!" "Let us see!"

"Hurry up, Ethan! What's the matter, Ethan?"

"Why are you so slow?"

"Doesn't she like it?"

Lily heard it downstairs. She was worn out with the whole affair. She put her hands to her ears and rushed out of the house. Neziah was at her elbow. "Come. You need refreshing."

An hour later, one of the guests, a matron who Lily had knows as a girl in Jerusalem, one of those who had twittered and whispered about the delights of the marriage bed, found the groom's mother in the kitchen. She was holding a small cup in one hand and a dried fig in the other.

"My dear Lily, I've been looking all over for you. Such marvelous food and so much of it! You must have worked yourself to the bone, yet you are as young and slim as a virgin."

The matron looked enviously at Lily's trim waist and patted her own swollen belly. "My time is soon, I hope, but there will be another in the womb before the year's out."

She paused. "Are you taking something for your stomach? I have a little indigestion myself. Give me some, please:"

Lily had a choking fit. Tamar came to the rescue. She brought forth a small cup of lentils stirred into wine. Both women exclaimed, "Tamar, you are a treasure!"

Chapter 10
Marriages

Judging by the silence and the amount of time that the bridal couple spent in bed that first of two weeks allotted for nuptials, Ethan must have heeded his mother's advice. He came down for meals occasionally, looking rumpled and self-conscious. Lily would send Tamar upstairs with food for the bride and queries as to whether she needed anything.

Tamar would return grinning and announce loudly, "She's as full of seed as a ripe gourd and as happy as a clam!"

Naarah finally ventured forth, quietly at first. The happy pair tried to act like old married people, but their exuberance would break forth. They would chase each other all over the house, and end the frolic in bed. They would sit at dinner, each using one hand to eat, the other under the table probing for more excitement. Suddenly they would spring up, and the chase would break out again. Sometimes they didn't make it back to their bed. They didn't care. Everyone smiled on young lovers, didn't they?

Jeduthun, however, was not amused. All the animal spirits, the pounding feet, the squeals and heavy breathing drove him out of the house. He found respite at the gathering place with men from Nippur who had come to honor Eleazar at his burial. There were three men in the delegation: a very old priest who had know Eleazar in Jerusalem, and two younger scribes who were interested in the scrolls kept by Eleazar. The four had much in common and spent long hours in deep discussion.

Jeduthun trued to persuade the ancient priest to stay and take Eleazar's place, but he would not. The young scribes tried to persuade Jeduthun to lend them the scrolls for copying, but he would not. It was explained that there was great activity downstream at Nippur. Scribes were collecting and carefully copying every document from the Temple that they could lay hands on. Not only that, but they were also calling all the old heads who could recall the stories of their forefathers to come and dictate what they had heard of Noah, Abraham, Lot, Jacob, and their womenfolk. The scribes had tales from people of Samaria, who called Yahweh El, the Almighty. They, too, knew about Adam and Eve and Cain and Abel.

"Nippur has a great school of scribes, who write in perfect Hebrew. You must join us, Jeduthun, and give us the words of the great hymns that you

Exile

know so well. The praises of Israel will be forgotten unless we make a record, or so Nunn says."

Before they returned to Nippur, Jeduthun had promised that "someday" he would join them in their great work, lest Jerusalem be not remembered in her glory. He told Lily about the plan, and she told Neziah.

They agreed that it was an excellent idea. "It would be a wonderful way for my father to get into that work and out of his despondency," murmured Lily into her lover's ear.

"Then you will come to be my wife openly? No more sneaking out? No more pretending?"

"Soon, soon. Naarah is learning the household duties, and surely she is with child. As soon as father settles down."

One night he came for her and had hardly handed her into the covered litter when she whispered excitedly, "Father is going to Nippur in two days. They have sent a boat for him."

In Neziah's boat they made love and plans. "I'll go to Jeduthun in the morning and tell him that my house awaits his daughter as its new mistress, my wife."

Bright and early the next morning Neziah presented himself at Jeduthun's house, followed by two litter bearers bringing lilies for Lily and a stack of sheets of papyrus for her father.

Jeduthun welcomed him warmly and thanked him for the valuable papyrus. "It will be most welcome at Nippur, for scribes never have enough."

"I must speak with you before you go. I seek the widow Lily in marriage."

"She is not a widow. She has a husband who went down into Egypt and may arrive here any day."

"Nobody has heard from him in all these years, Maestro. He must be dead."

"Lily knows no such thing. She is not free to remarry." Jeduthun spoke with finality.

"Lily could keep still no longer. "Father," she said calmly, "Neziah and I are husband and wife. We have lain together ever since..."

She was spared the half-lie she was about to tell by Jeduthun himself. She saw his face turn an ashen pallor, then as red as a beet, while the cords of his neck swelled angrily.

"Adulteress!" he roared. Then in an icy voice he plainly said, "Out of my sight! Out of my house! Begone! Let me not see you or your partner in sin again. Never!"

Neziah took Lily by the arm and half carried her to the waiting litter. "Now, now, don't cry. It will be all right in a few days. But we'll have the wedding feast at our house tonight."

They paused only a moment at the Hanan warehouse, just long enough to tell Likhi, the manager, to follow to the compound across the river. Neziah held his bride in his arms as they were rowed across and tried to calm her with kisses. Once there, he led her to her chamber and handed her over to her new maid. Adah, and the needlewomen. Lily was so dazed by the rapid turn of events that she was barely conscious that Neziah was issuing orders right and left, or that the needlewoman was eyeing her and measuring her for a gorgeous dress to be worn that night at the banquet.

Lily sank shivering onto the softest, most luxurious bed she had ever dreamed of. It was long and wide enough for all kinds of dalliances, and it was adorned with rich coverlids and piles of embroidered cushions.

"Would my lady have the red or the blue?" The sewing woman was showing her exquisite silks. Lily hesitated.

"The master suggests the crimson."

Lily quickly agreed and Adah, the maid, started to massage her mistress's body with salves and unguents. She worked them into the skin, soothing and perfuming, relaxing the overwrought woman who would rejoice with Neziah that night. She gave her a little poppy juice, which made Lily drowsily submissive to further mysteries of female beauty.

Ethan had left early for market with a pair of sandals. Returning later that morning he found a strangely quiet house.

"Where is everybody?" he yelled.

Naarah appeared and drew him into the privacy of their room. She told him that his mother and Neziah ben Hanan had been thrown out of the house for adultery and had presumably gone to the man's estate across the river.

"Lovers? But they are too old," he said.

"True nevertheless. I have seen Lily sneaking out after everyone else was in bed."

"You must be mistaken. They are so old. My mother..." He stopped short, remembering the lecture she gave him just before his marriage. Could it be...?

"Your grandfather has forbidden them to enter this house ever again. He is furious."

"Of course, Grandfather is right. This is his house. Adultery is forbidden by the law of Moses. At least he is not having her stoned."

Ethan sighed and waited anxiously for Jeduthun to come out of his music room. When he did appear for the evening meal, he seemed calm and deliberate.

"Ethan, my son, Naarah, my daughter." His deep voice caressed them and he looked fondly upon the two young people whom he had taught to sing, whom he had drilled and perfected. "I am packing to go to Nippur to join in a great undertaking—recording the heritage of Zion. I leave you here to promote and cherish the Sabbath music and the gathering of the remnants of our people in this community. Bring together more young people lest they forget Jerusalem. Teach the children to worship the one God of our fathers. Teach them how our Lord saved this people by His mighty hand

Exile

and outstretched arm. Let not the work of His servants, Moses and David, be lost in this idolatrous and filthy land."

The young couple gravely assented to the heavy charge laid upon them. "Yes, Grandfather, we will obey your instructions."

"I leave this house for your abode, yours and your children's. For good and sufficient reason I have forbidden Lily to come to this house. She carries the taint of Babylon. You and your children must not come near her lest you, too, be infected. Too many of the children of Jacob have succumbed to the fleshpots of the heathen. Let it not be so with you."

Ethan felt that the weight of Israel had been laid upon him but he cheered up when he learned that Jeduthun was leaving him a zither, a flute, and a horn with stops. Naarah shed a tear and then mentally started to rearrange the furniture.

The following day, Jeduthun, packed and ready to go, clasped his children and gave them his blessing. As he strode off to join the Nippur delegation he mused, "It is well for the old to move on and let the young take over their responsibilities." He dared not look back.

The ben Hanan wedding feast was possibly the most elaborate social affair in the reign of Nebuchadnezzar. It was certainly the most talked about. And so sudden, some added. Not so. Neziah had been planning the coming of Lily for years. Bunah, the steward, had his orders; the cooks had theirs; even the business people had been alerted through Likhi. So invitations sped throughout the wealthy Jewish community on the left bank, and operations in the market house were put on hold. Neziah had only to set in motion the organization that had made his fortune.

Lily yielded herself to the ministration of an expert cosmetician and a seamstress ranked high in Babylonian fashion circles. They and their assistants had been hired and retained by Neziah. They were now pleased to have a body worthy of their talents. They admired their lovely mistress, while they sought to make her even more delectable.

Late in the afternoon the bride stood before a long, copper mirror. She saw her blue-black hair elaborately plaited and piled up like a crown, held by golden combs and filets. Her dress was wrapped tightly around her slender body in diagonal folds that conformed to her jutting breasts and flat loins, but flared below the knee into a fringe through which peeked dainty ankles and feet encased in gilded sandals.

Lily was staring in amazement when her husband entered through the door to his room. He took her hand, kissed it, and said, "Come, beautiful wife. Our guests are arriving."

Each guest in turn was presented to a smiling Lily. Gracious formalizations of politeness were exchanged, and the host and hostess took their places, side by side, at a huge banqueting board that extended from the dining hall down the entire length of the inner courtyard. The guests followed and were served a great variety of meat stews—kid, pigeon, hearts and livers-cooked with blood and sour milk. There were dozens of puddings seasoned with cinnamon, ginger, and cloves, sweetened with honey. Mounds of peaches, plums, cherries, pomegranates, and grapes added color and cleared palates for the feast. Both date and grape wine flowed plentifully.

And while the company enjoyed this lavish fare, musicians played and dancing girls displayed their inviting charms in rhythm to small drums and ankle bells.

Heads began to turn and tongues to loosen in a deafening hubbub.

"No wonder father would not accept engagements at these feasts,," thought Lily, shocked that good Jews—pillars of society—would look upon such fleshy enticements. Yes, not only look, but look with avid relish.

She turned to her husband. He was talking with someone on his right. Lily overheard the word "Jerusalem." And so the big question was answered, person to person, down the table. When it hit one old matron, she snorted in disbelief. "Well, she didn't bring that dress from Jerusalem, that's certain. There was never such a getup in Jerusalem, even at the court of Solomon."

"Did you notice the gold threads in the fabric?" contributed her neighbor, whose ample neck was covered with gold chains. "More than in one piece my Abner refused to buy for me."

If there were thoughts that Neziah had found this gorgeous woman in some outlandish place, they were quickly suppressed, for the son of Hanan stood high in their admiration. He could do no wrong. And his wife would set the style and the pace. A great improvement over Ullah, they all agreed.

The dancers left. The guests rose from tables and sorted themselves into groups, men at one end of the hall, women at the other. The ladies buzzed about Lily with compliments and good wishes, interspersed with pointed questions about where she came from. She found herself saying over and over, "I was widowed in Jerusalem.." Her facial muscles began to ache (from holding that smile) and her shoulders began to droop.

Neziah was being slapped on the back by his friends at the other end of the room. "You sly fox! Where did you find that gorgeous woman?" He repeatedly answered, "She is a widow from Jerusalem." They queried the Babylonians in the party and, getting negative answers, were forced to conclude that Lily had arrived in the third deportation, too young for earlier arrivals to have known her.

Neziah saw that his bride was wilting under the strain. He caught Bunah's eye and summoned him with a jerk of the head as he strode across the room. "Help our friends make up their mind to go home." The steward understood that this meant cutting down on the wine, or watering it.

The master picked up his wife and stood in the doorway to her room. He said clearly, "Bride and bridegroom do not need your assistance. Thank you all. Good night!"

Exile

He whisked her across the threshold and bolted the door. Swiftly Lily's splendid red dress slid to the floor and was joined by Neziah's dazzling white linen tunic and cloak. He held his bride close and fondled her until her nervous tremors eased. The clamor in the house began to die down. When all was quiet they consummated their love, at last, at home in bed.

Next sunrise Lily awoke to find Neziah eyeing her critically as if she were a work of art. "Lovely, beautiful, exquisite, perfect. Stand, my wife, that your breasts may take their full shape."

Lily stood. Neziah turned her slowly, studying the loosened hair, the big black eyes, the straight nose, the rose petal lips slightly parted over white teeth. There was a slight irregularity, one upper front tooth touching lightly above the other. Lovely. He kissed the mouth and the hollow at th base of the throat. Delicious. The breasts stood out full and firm. The nipples had been painted scarlet. Irresistible. The tiny wine cup that was her navel. The pubic hair bright gold.

"How utterly charming," he said. "Do you realize that this is the first time I've been able to see your treasures?"

Lily looked at her painted nails and nipples and knew that Adah had skill of the highest order. She smiled up at Neziah.

"Now," said he, reaching between his legs and bringing forward his male appendages, "I am going to give you a present. Look, my love, they are yours."

Lily could not bring herself to look, but turned her head and averted her eyes.

"Don't play the bashful maiden with me. You have known and enjoyed my jewels for these many years. Now I give them to you and to you alone, my wife. Look at them."

Lily obediently directed her gaze to the swollen, pulsing testicles surmounted by the rearing penis. They were delicately colored, huge, and desirable.

"My husband, I accept your gracious gift; in return I give you, and you alone, my sheath for your dagger."

She drew him into her as she lay back on the bed.

"Ha!" said Neziah—the bride was wooing the groom in broad daylight.

Some time later, the bride roused herself with a start and saw the groom tying on a loin cloth.

"Cover yourself, you shameless hussy," he said with an appreciative twinkle in his eye. "I'll get some service in this room."

Lily dutifully pulled a coverlet over herself. He pulled it over her head. She made an aperture for one eye. Neziah left through the doorway to his room, clapped his hands to summon his body servant, Gomer. They quickly returned, followed by other servants bearing ewers of water and a big bowl. Still others brought in trays of fruit, cakes, and flagons of wines. They left as silently as they had come.

Neziah brought the bowl and a pitcher of water over to the bed and bathed his wife. In this act, so tender and so caring, Lily felt his great devotion to her and was moved to tears. He understood, and kissing them away whispered, "You are my love, my life. I need you. Always."

He washed himself and wrapped a large cotton square around his lower body. Then he wrapped Lily in another and they happily broke their fast with fruit and wine.

"Perhaps the sacred marriage of Ishtar and Marduk is like this?"

"Neziah, you bad boy—don't ever think of such heathen rites."

"Adam and Eve then?"

Lily reached for an apple and offered it to him.

"No, I prefer yours."

They spent the afternoon in exploration of all the erogenous spots each could find in the other. It was a delightful love game, full of surprises and satisfactions, tickles and wiggles, thrustings and withdrawings, heavy breathing and giggles; a very merry marriage bed. At last they slept.

The morning of their second day of marriage Neziah awoke to a vision of his bride covered with drops of bath water. They caught the rosy light of the rising sun and made Lily look so pink and delicious that he rushed to have her then and there. In his haste he could not get into position but covered them both with his semen.

"O Lily," cried Neziah in shame. "You have turned me into a green youth. I am so sorry...."

Lily smiled and said, "My turn to bathe us. A pity to waste so much."

Afterwards they wrapped themselves in cotton squares and spoke knowingly of David and Bathsheba. They argued about who had enticed whom and they played the roles laughingly, then seriously.

"I like being married," said Lily.

"The bed does beat the boat for making love," replied her husband.

"Isn't it wonderful that we can go on like this for two weeks? I could lie here forever."

"O, my very dear," Neziah pulling himself upon his elbows, said earnestly. "Again I am so sorry. I must tell you—tomorrow I must return to business. There are two caravans making ready to depart and one that came in as I was going to your house. These are weighty matters that require my attention. You'd not have us starve, would you?"

"Neziah, how can you leave me alone? I can't bear to be separated from you so soon." Lily's grief and fear seized her again.

Her husband comforted her. Haunted by the coming separation, they spent the afternoon in an orgy of libido.

The morning after, the morning of the third day, Neziah left before dawn with a kiss and a promise to return early. Lily drowsily felt aches and bruises and a conscience that bade her get up to her domestic duties. She drifted off to sleep.

She next awoke to find Adah clucking over her with healing pastes and ointments. "The master said you should rest abed today and let me minister to you."

And when the master returned in the late afternoon, he found his bride fresh and radiant in a sea-green gown with depths of blue. Her hair had been washed in sweet scented water, braided, and tied in a chignon. Over it he tossed a rope of pearls.

"A present for my love, the mistress of this house," he said, kissing Lily's hand and leading her into the dining hall.

There they sat, side by side, a dignified old married couple, while Bunah directed the serving of food. Lily nibbled. Neziah ate heartily but between bites he managed to whisper that he was eager to remove that fancy frock.

"I, too," whispered Lily. "When I heard you splashing about in your room I tried to enter, but Gomer stopped me."

He said, "Yes, dear. You must see me only in my white kilt and cloak, not dingy and grimy after a day's work in the market house."

"Except in bed, I hope."

"Of course. Say, this meal has gone on too long. Let's go!"

Seizing a wing jug and goblet, he took them and his bride to their private quarters.

Next morning Lily made herself arise to take up her household duties. Shortly after Neziah left, she called for the simple duncolored tunic she had worn when she came. She tied her hair in a white scarf. No more fancy clothes while she went about her work. Dressing up was for night and Neziah.

The good little Jewish housewife inspected the kitchen, where she found many idlers; the weaving house, where she found idle looms; the orchards, the gardens which she found full of weeds; the washing pools, where the women made merry with a huge Nubian water carrier. Bunah, accompanying his mistress, could find excuses for everything.

Tactfully and in small bits, Lily told her husband her ideas. He promptly told Bunah, "Your mistress' wish is my law. Obey her."

But he could not help being amused about the water bearer. "What's so odd about a gourd? I wear one myself at business."

The water bearers were soon covered by half-skirts, the idlers put to weaving, gardeners were found, and a woman skilled in processing herbs. Neziah rejoiced to find that his residential property was made to pay for itself without in the least diminishing the passion of its mistress. And few of the dozens of employees could imagine that the ordinary woman, who inspected their work every morning with the steward, was the goddess who enthralled their master every night. For, her domestic duties completed, Lily returned to her room and allowed Adah to take over the beautification of her body.

Rachel Stern

Her gaze would wander idly over the colorful glazed tiles of the walls, the thick carpets that adorned the less elaborate bricks of the floor, the piles of elegant cushions on the bed where she lay. But her thoughts and her desires were for Neziah and for their night together. The copper mirror, the ceramic bathtub, the elegant dresses all served only one purpose: Neziah.

Chapter 11
Scholars

Babylon in the time of Nebuchadnezzar straddled the life-giving waters of the Euphrates. The great king, proud of his piety, boasted of enlarging and embellishing the more modest buildings of his father, Nabupolassar. Both men sought to restore the city to its former grandeur and to glorify its god Marduk above all other gods. Thus Babylon became the center and wonder of the world to the heathen. To the Jews, the great city was the sink of iniquity and the flail of God's wrath laid upon His disobedient people.

On the west bank of the river lay the garden estates of the wealthy, like the Hanans, who wished to escape the noise and dirt of the older city on the east bank. The Hanans had lived there when they first arrived in the houses they later gave to their compatriots, Jeduthun and Eleazar. They kept their trading operations in their east bank quarter, commuting across river by light boats oared by strong men who knew the currents and the traffic.

The Euphrates was the main highway going from the mountains in the north to the Lower Sea in the south. It was, however, a treacherous life giver, for its users never knew when it would flood, run low, or silt up and change course. Mesopotamia was thus a land laced with canals, the maintenance of which required not only knowledge and direction, but also political organization. Canals served to divert flood waters, store water for tillage in time of drought, and to carry goods to markets. Nebuchadnezzar made a great canal and moat a vital part of the fortification of his city. Reaching from the Ishtar Gate to the Euphrates bridge, a canal centered on the Processional Way separated the palace and temple enclave from the noise and dust of the commercial city.

Jeduthun had never set foot within Babylon's temple-palace precinct. He averted his eyes from it and moved only in the Jewish quarter. Yet he felt a deepening sense of loss when he left the despised city, for he left behind the few ties to his former life that remained to him: his grandson and his daughter. Still, he hoped he left behind the shame they had brought to him. He, therefore, left them voluntarily to find a place of peace and a task to which he could devote his remaining years. He carried his scrolls, a sampling of instruments, and his musical memory to Nippur. He swallowed his pride and included Neziah's gift of papyrus.

Nippur was not what it had been in old Babylonian times—a seat of learning where many scribes taught their pupils and built up a vast library of clay tablets. Nebuchadnezzar, in his zeal to honor the past, had restored ancient buildings and encouraged settlement, but the river had abandoned Nippur and pleasure-loving Babylonians found it dull. So it was that many able Jews, carried away by Nebuchadnezzar, found houses and fields south of Babylon ready for them. And there, like the ancient Sumerians, they set up an important scribal school to record and transmit the heritage of Israel. The writing place was attached to their gathering place; both were generously supported by the farmers and merchants of the area.

Jeduthun was greeted with warm appreciation into this community, which he found much more interested in poetry and music than the languishing group at Eleazar's house in the Street of the Shoemakers. The choir master of Nippur immediately invited the great musician of the Temple, more lately wasting his talents in Babylon, to select from the singing men and singing women his own choir. Jeduthun was so touched by this gift that his loneliness gave way to gratitude. He wept to know that there were still some who valued him.

Two mature, but youngish men came to him and bowing said, "Hazan, may we have the honor of serving as your scribes?"

Jeduthun smiled, thanked them, and replied, "But I don't need a scribe. I can write, if need be. But I teach music by imitation and memory. It was so in Jerusalem, and I do not change in Babylonia."

The two men bowed and withdrew.

Jeduthun went to the writing place and saw that there was a great project underway. At long tables men bent over the meticulous copying of ancient scrolls. Some were writing on vellum; others on papyrus sheets, which would later be attached to and wound on scrolls. Below men were preparing the vellum, scraping away every vestige of hair. Above were stacks of material, used or ready for use. The process was demanding at every stage, for not a jot or a tittle could be amiss. Jeduthun had to admit to himself that age had dimmed his eyes and stiffened his hands; he was no longer a ready scribe. The Levite in charge, a son of Zephan, invited Jeduthun to participate. He would furnish him a scribe who could take dictation as soon as one was free. Jeduthun was honored and said so.

The next day the two scribes who had offered their services before again presented themselves.

"We are brothers, Sherah and Tahath. We are here to fulfill the last command of our mother. She said we must 'find Jeduthun.' She died recently, but always spoke highly of you. She knew you in Jerusalem."

"Her name?"

"Delilah."

"No, I did not know anyone of that name in Jerusalem. But I shall be needing a scribe, I am told. Your father's name?"

"Eber. But he died long ago when we were small children."

"I'm sorry but I do not recognize that name either. But then my life has been spent in musical circles. I must have a scribe who can take dictation for songs that have not yet been written down. A great many, I'm afraid."

"O maestro, we can take the word as you speak or sing. We know something of music, too. We will be honored to record the high poetry of Israel from the lips of Jeduthun, and we will write perfectly in two copies. We always write together, one going over the writing of the other."

Jeduthun hesitated before he said, "I may not be allowed two scribes."

"If you ask, you will be given. We earnestly entreat you for our mother's sake."

The singer and his scribes settled in at the writing place before the stack of papyrus sheets, the gift of Neziah. Jeduthun had other duties with his choir, his pupils, and his singing engagements. Time passed so quickly that he rarely thought of Babylon.

Occasionally he joined the priests as they studied the old scrolls and tried to figure out who wrote them. This was an august council composed of descendants of Aaron, men of understanding, learned in the wisdom of the scrolls long kept in Jerusalem. Jeduthun was particularly interested when the council of priests (under the direction of Azariah, son of Hilkiah) took up the question of authorship of a love song attributed to Solomon. It promised to be a lively debate, expert witnesses having been called in from all the exile communities in Babylonia. Jeduthun suggested that his scribes, Sherah and Tahath, lift their heads from their copying and get a broader view of Hebrew literature.

Jeduthun gravely took a high seat in the council chamber, looked across to the crowded benches on the opposite side, and saw his two scribes nodding and bowing to attract his attention. He returned their greeting and suddenly realized that he had rarely looked at their faces bowed as they were over their copying. Their merry eyes somehow seemed vaguely familiar.

He looked to the end of the room where an old woman was alternately speaking and intoning what purported to be the wisdom of Solomon:

> "*Go to the ant, thou sluggard...Pride goeth before destruction ... Can a man take fire in his bosom and his clothes not be burned?*"

These proverbs of our great king Solomon show that his mind lay upon prudence...."

It was dull and heavy stuff. Jeduthun's attention wandered and his gaze fell upon Sherah and Tahath. There was something truly familiar about them. The old woman went on:

"Is it likely that a man who had more than three hundred wives and concubines would go mooning over a woman? No! This is what he had to say about women, the perfect woman:

> 'She worketh willingly with her hands...'
> 'She riseth also while it is yet night, and giveth meat to her household and a portion to her maidens.'
> 'She girdeth her loins with strength, and strength with her arms...'

"No! That's not the woman of the Song. Solomon's woman only opened her mouth with wisdom. Would she go to the gates, where her husband sat and talked with the elders of the land, and entice him to lie with her in that vineyard she had bought and planted?"

The old crone was making a foolish display of her learning and a mockery of the wisdom of the great Solomon. Jeduthun was bored. He let his attention wander to his two bright-eyed scribes. They teased his memory.

Suddenly he heard a glorious voice pouring out golden notes that shimmered, soared, and transformed the drab council chamber. Jeduthun's skin tingled as he responded to the sweetness of the sound. It was Naarah Ethan's wife, whose fresh and vibrant voice he had trained. Of course! That old bore was her grandmother. Evidently Azariah thought she was knowledgeable in the oral traditions of Israel and had sought her advice on grave matters. But what was that frivolous, kittenish girl Naarah doing here?

She was singing from the *Song* with all the allure and the enticement intended by the author:

"Let us get up early to the vineyards; let us see if the vines flourish, whether the tender grapes appear and the pomegranates bud forth: There will I give thee my love ...all manner of pleasant fruits, new and old, which I have laid up for thee, O my beloved."

There was more. The old woman would sound the sour notes of *The Preacher* and the young one would counter with anatomical erotica:

"Thy navel is like a round goblet, which wanteth not liquor. Thy belly is like ...Thy two breasts are like..."

Jeduthun was shocked, horrified. He was not the only one. The audience cleared throats and shuffled feet with increasing impatience until Azariah called a halt.

"O sage woman of old Judea, we see that you do not think Solomon wrote the passionate poem, though his name appears at the end. You have spoken eloquently and lengthily, you and your young pupil. Now will you tell us briefly—instruct us in as few words as possible—just who in your opinion did write the song attributed to Solomon? One word, if possible."

The sage stood straight, squared her shoulders, and uttered two words: "Solomon's mother!"

The elders of Zion rose and, as one, let out a roar of outrage. Bathsheba! It was shameful. It was an insult! Drive out the evil witches!

Exile

The two women fled. Jeduthun wanted to follow them to inquire about Ethan and, yes, Lily, but he was ashamed of being found with such singers. He was the last man to leave the room. Outside he found his scribes waiting for him, and he asked which way the women went.

"Toward the canal, Maestro. They had a boat waiting."

"They were covered with confusion and shame, I am sure."

"On no, sir. They were dying laughing."

Jeduthun's memory took another jog. Merry eyes under a yellow scarf… "Humph;" he said aloud and to himself. "It isn't possible."

Chapter 12
Naarah and Ethan

Naarah's brilliant performance at Nippur reflected her love life with Ethan back home in Babylon. She and Ethan romped and played and coupled like animals in heat, but, unlike animals, in all seasons. No matter about babies in the bed or in the womb, the two young people lived in a libidinous daze enhanced by the Song, which Naarah learned for her grandmother's testimony. She would croon to him about the delights which she offered his desires. Ethan quickly learned the responses, not just the words. Together they experienced the poem as the chief joy in an otherwise dull existence.

Ethan's shoe making was hardly a commercial success. With Naarah always in his mind, he would make exquisite, fragile shoes instead of the sturdier sandals and boots that found ready sale. Tamar, who usually could find no fault with her lusty "boy," worried about the bare larder and knew that they would go hungry if it were not for occasional offerings from the meeting place or more regularly from a strange servant who Tamar was sure came from Neziah. Atab had departed to get regular work digging out canals for the Babylonians.

Nine months after the wedding, the bride gave birth to a fine son, whom they named Shama and had circumcised by a traveling priest. Before she could bring her offering and be cleansed, Naarah was again with child. And again she gave Ethan a fine son, whom they named Sabtah.

The third and fourth years of their marriage, however, were marred by a series of still births, miscarriages, and wasting illness. Naarah was a shadow of her former self and her voice a whisper. Tamar brought in a second Jewish midwife, who could do nothing. Another, a Babylonian woman of great and expensive repute, came and spoke to Ethan with none of the deference due to the man of the house.

"You must not lie with your wife. Do not even touch her, lest your seed kill her. Sleep elsewhere or she will die."

Ethan, abashed, paid the woman with his last pair of shoes, and spent the next two nights in his grandfather's old room. It was so lonely. He made up a cot in Naarah's chamber so that they could talk. It was so cold. Their need for each other overrode caution. The former behavior ensued as night to day.

Exile

Here stood Ethan, age twenty-one, weighted down with a load of care: a family of two toddling babies and an ailing wife, a languishing shoe business, a faltering and diminishing choir the only means of support. How could he feed them and hold up his head as chief musician as his grandfather had done? He longed to feel his grandfather's strong hand holding his and guiding him. He longed for his mother's shoulder to weep on. His handsome face and his youthful limbs concealed a heart frozen with fear.

It was in this situation that Ethan first became involved with some ladies of Babylon who scandalized the Jews: they lay about on temple steps, offering sex for no price or a very small gift. Ethan was ware of his breaking the law of Moses, but it did give his wife a respite.

Thus it was that before he had completed his twenty-second year in this world, he had added to his burdens the guilt of sin, a sickly baby who cried and wailed, and a sickly wife who wept from weakness over her tiny girl.

Ethan walked woodenly to the great market, where his guild of cobblers kept a stall. It was his turn to man it, but he had no heart for his trade: the returns were far short of his need to pay wet nurses and midwives, to say nothing of food and clothing. He could not ask for help from Lily and Neziah, whom he had turned away repeatedly, citing Jeduthun's orders. He would not go to Jeduthun, who had left him his house, his instruments, and his office at the meeting place. No. It would break his grandfather's heart to see Ethan a failure. He could not and would not. Jehovah? He had paid his dues to Ishtar.

The young man entered the stall, put down his few sandals, greeted the man he was relieving.

"Peace. Is business better?"

"So so. See you next week."

Ethan busily rearranged the stock of sandals, boots, and shoes. He brought forward some of the prettiest and most elaborate, his own work, all unsold. He sat, his head in his hands, utterly discouraged.

"Who made these slippers?" It was a sharp Babylonian voice speaking Aramaic.

Ethan recognized in the man's hands the only pair he had sold in three months. "I made them. What's wrong? I'll fix, but not take back."

"They do not fit my mistress perfectly. She wants another pair that does fit. You are to come to take her measurements and her order."

"As you see, I cannot leave the booth."

"My mistress will pay more than you can make in this booth all week. Come now. I'll show you the way."

While Ethan and his guide picked their way through the trash of back streets, they conversed in the trade language of the region, Aramaic. Ethan, in a desire to give himself more importance than the Babylonian servant was willing to allow, stated that he was a singer, chief musician, and maker of instruments like his grandfather, who was formerly famous in Jerusalem. The servant was duly impressed. Nevertheless, they entered a palace through a back gate and went through a maze of courtyards before Ethan was told to wait.

The young Jew gazed in wonder at the spaciousness, the richness that surrounded him. Polished stones, carefully cut and laid, paved the area. Had he not heard of such stones in the house of the Most High in Jerusalem? Where had a resident of Babylon, a city of mud bricks, obtained such stones? The walls were covered with glazed tiles in brilliant colors arranged in rows and patterns. The work was of the kind seen by the public only at the Ishtar Gate. Ethan could not guess and never did find out just where in relation to the Sacred Way this house was located. Was it the home of an important priest or of some member of Nebuchadnezzar's family? Important people undoubtedly came in from the front on Procession Street—as some called the wide, fortified Sacred Way but this cobbler-singer knew only the back gate and that after threading a jumble of twisting lanes.

He was summoned to enter a big room partitioned by hangings of linen. These were kept wet and moved to and fro by slaves. They partially concealed the brilliant tiles of the walls, and cooled the blistering heat of Babylonian summer. His guide brought him up to one of several ladies lolling about on cushions and spoke with her briefly. The lady Arissi was a thin woman in her middle years who amused herself with clothes and younger men. She looked with favor at the handsome Hebrew and motioned him to sit beside her. Ethan saw her black dress, tiers of deep flounces, her golden hairnet, and her black eyes rimmed with kohl. They were flirting eyes, and he gave back an arch and appreciative look.

She handed him a harp, the handsomest he had ever seen, inlaid with ivory figures and mounted on an ivory bull's head.

Ethan strummed, tightened string, and played an elaborate introduction. What should he sing? The Song of Solomon, which he thought very funny in spite of Naarah's obsession with it, gave a starting point for one of his improvisations:

> *"How beautiful are thy feet in shoes, O princess' daughter…*
> *Hidden from the eyes of man are the colors of thy soles.*
> *Thine arches spring from toe to heel unseen by the heart that*
> *springs upon you.*
> *How perfect are thy feet in shoes, old woman."*[17]

Ethan's tenor crooned like a caress. The woman winked at him and laughed knowingly, though she did not understand a word of his perfect Hebrew.

> *"More beautiful are thy feet in sandals, O alluring old goat.*
> *Thy toes peep forth like tender buds of roses in a garden of mandrakes.*
> *How shall I find thy love if thou art shod?"*[17]

Ethan leered and ogled, gleefully playing the part of a moonstruck youth, and let his voice fall to a suggestive whisper.

Arissi dismissed her women and stood before him to have her feet measured. On a square of cloth he outlined her left and was marking the right, when down came a black flounce. He brushed it aside. Down came another, and another, a torrent of flounces. He raised his head and was faced by the international invitation that knows no language barrier.

When she had done with him, she told one of the slaves who had all the while been fanning them with a damp curtain to fetch the usher. He led a dazed and disheveled Ethan through the many courtyards to the back entrance. There he gave Ethan a purse of small silver coins, Nebuchadnezzar's new minting just coming into general circulation. He also gave instructions:

"Come tomorrow to give music lessons to my lady's daughter, Adelia. She must have entertainment while her parents negotiate her marriage. She has learned Hebrew and Sumarian for the songs. A very knowing maiden. The pay is good, as you see. Come early and be prepared to stay as long as you are needed."

Ethan stumbled home, gave the purse to Tamar, who accepted it thankfully without question. She sent him to Naarah's bedside with a bowl of soup. He did not lie with her that night. Or the next. Or the next.

The "very knowing maiden" proved to be a fat girl just entering puberty with more lust than love for music. A few minutes of song sufficed to introduce the frantic coupling that she craved. Ethan wondered about her future husband: "He will not find you a virgin."

"Virgin? What's that?"

"A young girl who has not had intercourse."

"Never heard of such a sad thing. I guess we girls would not put up with being virgins."

"But your husband should be the first...."

"They like us well-broken and practiced...."

Ethan gave up on the prudish law and went on doing the best he could with what he had in the heathen culture of Babylon.

The baby Alhai fattened when provided with a nourishing nurse. Naarah, however, wasted to skin and bones, took little food, and shivered in the sweltering heat of summer. One night Ethan carried her to the roof for a bit of cool air. She held his hand and confided, "My beloved, I fear I shall never live to see our daughter grow up or find pride in our sons. The day will soon come when I shall be gathered to my fathers and see you no more."

Ethan wept, for he feared the same.

"Let us then remember the days of our youth."

They cheered each other by recalling little incidents of their shared past.

Naarah was spurred by those recollections. "No. I cannot relinquish this life. I'll make a brave effort."

"Anthing. Anything, Naarah. Do not leave me."

The next day she had a long and serious consultation with the cleverest midwife in the city. She was advised that certain things could be done with tiny hooks on long needles. There might be fatal complications. Naarah told her to go ahead immediately.

When Ethan returned he found his wife in shock. Before going into coma she managed to whisper, "My dear, we are going to be lovers again. We won't have to worry." That night a raging fever burned her. There were chills at dawn and more fever. The midwife did her best with cloths and potions. Tamar bustled about trying to keep the children quiet. Not that Naarah cared. She was beyond noticing anything but pain.

Ethan was beside himself with grief. He did not eat. He did not leave the house. He had been through much with Naarah's previous birthings, but there was a feeling of doom about this illness; a searing loneliness that brought him to his knees facing Jerusalem, pleading for mercy from the God of his fathers, who had brought him up.

"Save, Lord, for Thy name's sake..."

Naarah fought for her life but showed no signs of improvement. Days and nights merged into a blur. Ethan left her bedside and went into Jeduthun's room, which faced west towards Jerusalem. He was calm, resigned to deserved punishment. And he prayed a song of repentance:

> *"Against Thee, Thee only, have I sinned.*
> *According to Thy tender mercies, blot out my transgressions.*
> *Purge me with hyssop, and I shall be clean...*
> *Hide Thy face from my sins, and blot out all mine iniquities.*
> *Create in me a clean heart, O God; and renew a right spirit within me...*
> *O Lord, open Thou my lips: and my mouth shall show forth Thy praise.*
> *For Thou desirest not sacrifices; else would I give it: Thou delightest not in burnt offerings.*
> *The sacrifices of God are a broken spirit: a broken and a contrite heart, O God, Thou wilt not despise."*[18]

That night Naarah's fever broke, and the next morning she greeted Ethan with a clear-eyed smile. "You prayed for me, and the Most High heard your prayer; all praise and thanks...."

Ethan did not correct her.

The word spread among the backsliding Jewish community that the petitions of Ethan had found favor in the ears of the Lord; his wife had been miraculously healed. People in distress came to the old gathering place asking the son of Jeduthun to carry their petitions in song, to repeat what he had said for Naarah. They brought offerings. The word went far and wide that the mantle of David had fallen upon the young praise-singer. Up and down the Euphrates Jews rejoiced that they once again had an advocate to speak for them.

Maybe with time he could speak to them for God. They needed a prophet, too, in their profound discouragement. Through the wasted years the bones had not risen. At Nippur, Ethan's fame rejoiced his grandfather. And the Council of Elders sent a priest to help him build up the congregation started by Eleazar and Hanan in that cesspool of sin, Babylon.

Ethan set his prayer to music. It became so popular that the author was forgotten: it was worthy of David and attributed to him. And though later priests edited and embellished it, the psalm still serves the human heart in its need to touch the heart of God.

---

[17] Song of Solomon 7
[18] Psalms 51

Chapter 13
Lily and Neziah

Lily quickly adapted to her new position as Neziah's wife. The close supervision she brought to the workforce resulted in both economy and better production: the washing was cleaner, the food tastier, the weaving smoother, and the gardening more fruitful. The beautiful house was less dusty, so the glazed tiles and inlaid furniture showed their bright colors, delighting the eyes.

She knew that she had married a wealthy man but had no idea of how rich ben Hanan was. The one thing that impressed her was the quantity of cotton squares. In varying sizes they were everywhere: at dining tables, by the bath and the voiding stool, and the bed. They required much time of the washer-women and much space on the berry bushes where they were dried. They were expensive, Lily knew, for she had once tried to buy just one small piece. The price in the bazaar had shocked her, and the merchant had explained: the soft material was very hard to spin and weave; it came from the wool tree that grew up north where only a few skilled women knew the secret of weaving it. Now Lily was mistress of hundreds of cotton cloths. She decided to mark them with the Hanan initial.

Her afternoons were spent on her bed with Adah bathing, anointing, and making her ready for the evening with Neziah. They would have a formal dinner together, Bunah serving, and then retire to their chamber for more intimate exchanges. The husband found his wife delicious and delightful and could hardly wait to get home to share with her news of the market place, or the court, or the Jewish community or whatever else would pique her intelligent curiosity and bring forth her lively comments. Their lovemaking fell into comfortable and confident routines. If he felt tired after a hard day of bargaining, he would say, "Woo me, my love." But mostly he did the wooing. Seldom was she coy.

Neziah issued strict orders that he was not to be interrupted while in his wife's chamber. He had a horror of coitus interruptus. Only one thing, and one thing only, was sufficient cause to break in upon his precious time with his wife: the arrival of his ship at port on the Lower Sea.

He explained to Lily that the ship was a serious and risky venture he had undertaken several years before. Under a Phoenician captain, it was to trade from the Red Sea, down its eastern shore, up and around Arabia, bringing ivory, gold and spices to the confluence of the two rivers at Basra. Neziah did not think the channel to the sea was deep enough for his ship to enter the Euphrates in low water, and so he had a plan to off-load and bring the cargo to Babylon in smaller boats. Since a large part of his fortune was involved, he was anxious about the outcome and must supervise the whole operation.

In the absence of the ship they made love. Summer heat turned to winter cold, necessitating braziers for warmth and a fur sleeping bag. Again came summer's dust, and still Lily's belly was a flat as such delightful flesh can be. She would say every now and then, "Neziah, I want to give you a son."

"Why? We have sons who are busily begetting sons." Or, after a particularly pleasurable orgasm, she would say, "Surely I conceived that time."

"If you are with child, I can't get to you. Who needs 'em?"

Or again, "I don't want to have to pull a squalling brat off your nipples when I want to sip."

"Well, sip, my love, but get me with child."

Years passed without any signs of the child or of the ship. Lily wanted to visit Ethan and her father. Neziah made regular inquiry and regularly advised her that she would not be received. He also had baskets of fish delivered to Ethan's house and to the gathering place. This pleased Lily, for one of her favorite projects was to put the old folk on the compound to fishing in the river.

"Be patient, my dear. In time they will be our friends again. Now they hurt, but time will heal," he comforted her.

But Lily felt a desperate need for a son to consummate her second marriage. A barren woman was nothing.

One night as they lay sleeping in each other's arms came loud cries and pounding on the door.

"The ship! Master, the ship! It has been sighted. It is almost in. The ship!"

Neziah sprang to the alert. Lily, awake and knowing her man, was determined not to show how she dreaded separation from him. She simply kissed him good-bye and gave the wifely warning to be careful.

"It will take a moon, maybe longer. I'll think of you every minute and return as soon as I can. Take care of my wife!" Neziah said to the servants as he flung on his clothes and hastened to his waiting boat at the jetty.

Lily felt sorry for herself during the remaining hours of that night, but with the dawn she pulled herself together and resumed her management of the domestic affairs of a man of far-flung enterprises. She dressed, breakfasted lightly on fruit and barley porridge, made her inspection tour, came home for a nap and a massage, bathed and dressed for dinner, ate in solitary splendor with an occasional word to Bunah, the steward. In her room on her lonely bed, she wept.

The routine was maintained for a week. Or was it two weeks? She tried to relieve her boredom with new projects: reed drying racks for the laundry;

overhead fans in the weaving room; a new and very seductive dress for Neziah's return. There was no escaping the fact that she missed Neziah. And it was not just as a bedfellow: she missed intelligent conversation, the news of the big outside that only a man brings home. She wanted to share his thinking on everything. She was alone, a hollow shell without him.

She resumed wishing: Neziah, a son by him; that would be real happiness. Her living son, Ethan; she would go to see him tomorrow. She pictured his welcome and her arms around him, the joy of it. Then she pictured a cold rejection. No. He wouldn't. Maybe soon.

So it was that one hot day Lily told Adah to prepare for a trip to the bazaar in Babylon. She would buy shoes. Summon a boat and a litter, both with canopies for protection against the sun. "Veils, too, of course. You will go with me."

"Bunah might be a help, my lady."

"No! No men servants." Lily had good reason to avoid unnecessary links with her past. Whore! She still smarted from the whispers and the rest of the sad story. She would spy out the ground first.

The two women, heavily veiled, were rowed across the river to the Hanan wharf, where they entered a covered litter. The bearers were told to go to shoe stalls. Coming up to one, Lily examined several pairs of fancy footwear.

"Not what I'm looking for. Try another place."

The next offerings were too big.

"Let's try over there." It was the booth that Ethan's guild maintained. She liked a pair of sandals but did not see Ethan. Conversation with the seller brought forth a flood of information about their most talented shoemaker.

"A great singer, too. He is so much in demand that he doesn't do much cobbling now. But I am sure he'd make something special for you, Madam, if you can wait until he has time."

"Where does he live?"

The man pointed at an opening in the jumble of houses. Lily took charge of directing the litter bearers so that her former home was quickly found. Ethan, who was expecting a pupil, opened the door.

Lily parted her veil and said one word:

"Ethan." Her voice carried years of yearning.

He slammed the door in her face.

Lily lay on her bed for the next few days, alternately burning and freezing. She refused food and sent Adah out so that she could weep in peace. Adah reported to the other servants that the heat had been too much for their mistress and perhaps she was with child. That uppity shoemaker turned singer, hadn't helped any with his rudeness.

"The hard heart," wept Lily. "How could he forget the years I cared for him? How could he be so cruel to his mother?"

Ethan, so understanding of his own sins, was bitter about the woman who had brought disgrace on the family. "The presumption! On top of shame," he muttered. "She deserves stoning or drowning."

A week later a messenger from Neziah came up river and reported first to Lily.

"The master is well. His business is good. His return has been delayed because of unexpected but favorable complications. He will leave for home as soon as possible."

The message helped Lily mend. She once more went about her duties and new projects: a stick on the wet rags used on dusty floors would not only keep down the dust but also save the backs of the servants.

At night she turned to prayer. Facing west toward Jerusalem, she no longer besought the Almighty for the sons she did not have. She thanked Him for what she did have: a good man's love.

Much lay behind Neziah's message from Basra, and all the way home he debated with himself about how much he should tell Lily.

He had arrived at the port just in time to keep the captain from selling part of the cargo, so great was the load of ivory. There were fortunes to be made in that commodity alone—great tusks taller than a man—to say nothing of the precious woods and spices and jewels. Neziah was more than pleased with his captain's venture, and promised him an extra share of the profits. The ship would stand well off shore, under armed guard, until its heaviest treasurers could be put into smaller boats to carry them through the shallow canals and sandy marshes to the main stream.

As the two men walked to the town's main caravansary, the captain added, "One more object have I brought, a piece of human wreckage. He found me in Akaba, on the Red Sea, and indicated that I bring him to you. As he carried your seal on a rare stone and said you had sent him to Egypt on confidential business, I let him come aboard and lie among the bales. He was too feeble to pull an oar, and he got worse on the long voyage."

"Yes! Yes! Go on!"

"I hope I did what you would want: I got him a corner in the inn and had a doctor come to him...."

Neziah ran the rest of the way. He found his spy Amok, half dead, lying in a bundle of rags, his eyes glazed with pain and fever. Making an effort, Amok focused on Neziah and said, "Jarib is..." and fell into a coma. Neziah called for the best physician in town, arranged for more comfortable quarters and constant attendance on the sick man. He sat beside him all that night, waiting for the report he had struggled so hard to deliver.

The doctor said that it might be days or even weeks before Amok would regain consciousness. Meanwhile, he would do the best he could. But this man had not only been beaten and bound, he had an evil flux in the blood, a purple death that was creeping all over him. Neziah saw the gangrene and choked with pity.

In the days of waiting that followed, Neziah had opportunity to converse with the doctor about the state of his profession. He learned about his brother, who specialized in the treatment of genitals.

"Very, very busy. Lots of sailors, you know."

While Neziah was not a sailor and had no complaint about his appendages, he did have a nagging suspicion that he might be getting a bit old for his ardent young wife. How she wanted a son! He decided to consult the specialist.

The very thought of that experience on the way home made his gorge rise. The indignity of it! How could he have let himself get into the hands of such a coarse brute. He had had no inkling of it as he entered the clinic and saw the dignified doctor in his purple, red, and green robes and peaked hat. His ponderous voice and haughty manner were those of a Chaldean sage, learned in all the wisdom of the East. Neziah was so impressed that he allowed himself to get into a situation of such degradation and humiliation that he never spoke of it to anyone. He had had to stay overnight so that a great cow of a woman could draw sperm at different hours. He figured that he must have been fed poppy juice.

The doctor summoned him at midmorning. He was in a jocular mood and without his impressive robes. Neziah cleared his head enough to hear him say:

"My dear fellow, you have the finest organs I have ever seen: Large, perfect, and abounding in seed. Don't waste them on a barren woman. Get yourself wives and concubines and raise up another tribe of Jacob."

Neziah paid and left in disgust. Obviously that mongrel of a doctor had no blood of Judah in his veins.

Returning to the inn, he found that his confidential agent had taken a sudden turn for the better. He had regained consciousness and was trying to speak.

Neziah sat with the dying man throughout that day and into the night. With pain and between gasps, the spy whispered his story. There were long intervals during which the doctor worked over his patient, who kept slipping back into oblivion. What Neziah learned was brief and incomplete, but he was reassured by it and felt that he could confirm to Lily what he had always maintained: she was a widow from the very beginning of their lovemaking in the barge.

The substance of Amok's report was that he had finally located Jarib in a Jewish settlement on the upper reaches of the Nile. No, he had not spoken to him because the Egyptian boat master who brought him was under armed guard, as were the Jews who brought gold and ivory from the interior to Pharoah's priests. The Jews were kept as prisoners to trade with the fierce natives of the Sudan and then sold only to the Egyptians. Yes, Amok had seen

Jarib, pointed out by the boatman. He was flourishing, had many black wives and scores of brown children. That was the way of it above the second cataract. Amok had had bad luck on the way out. Caught by slave traders, he had been bought and sold several times and was so broken by hardship that he was abandoned as useless on the approach to Akaba.

The spy Amok died that night. Neziah did not wait for dawn to order his swiftest boat and start up the Euphrates. He passed many of his own heavily laden barges. But even so, the pace was too slow and he took an oar, wielded it furiously, and tried to sort out the whole experience. They did not pause at night, but by taking on relays of rowers, made the ben Hanan warehouse jetty in four days. After an hour with Likhi, the accountant and manager, Neziah crossed the river in silence to surprise his wife.

Lily was beginning to dress for a lonely dinner. She thought she heard a little splashing in Neziah's room. It must be her wishful thinking, a bad habit she strove to overcome. And suddenly there he was! Neziah, bathed and combed, his bare arms outstretched, picked up his wife and put her on the bed. Neither spoke. Dinner was late that night.

During the meal, the returned traveler entertained the stay-at-home with an account of his mission to Basra. Returning to their room he said politely, "Now tell me about what you've been doing in my absence."

Lily started to comply, but before she could finish the first sentence, Neziah was sound asleep, exhausted. She looked at her dear man with eyes of love and the smile of the beloved. So, propped on one elbow, she passed the night until the flame in the lamp died.

In this serene hour Jarib, whom they thought safely penned up, broke out of his bondage in Egypt.

Summer heat and dust began to give way to winter rain and wind. Lily busied herself preparing the house for the change of seasons: the bitumen-covered clothes on rollers at doors and windows had to be recoated; charcoal for the braziers and oil for the lamps must be bought and stored; heavy clothing to replace summer garments was brought forth, aired and mended. Neziah had his hands and his hours full at his market house. But as the days grew shorter, he came home earlier. He and his wife had time to share their thoughts and their tastes, their fears and their dreams. They grew into one person, alike in ways that were important to their union, but with enough differences (and secrets) to add spice. They not only loved but also liked each other. 'Twas a cozy winter within their home while foul weather roared and poured without.

Spring came, renewing life, the New Year a celebration in itself. Akitu, the spring festival, had to be celebrated in Babylon with all the rites and pomp inherited from the ancient worship of the gods, plus Nebuchadnezzar's sumptuous elaborations for the chief god, Marduk, the almighty who won the king's battles. Marduk, the city god of fertility, who opened the womb and brought prosperity.

The month of Nissan saw the metropolis in a frenzy of activity centered at Marduk's temple, Esagila. Here the priests opened the lofty gates, purified themselves with Euphrates water and sprinkled the vast buildings and courtyards with Tigris water. Musicians played on their stringed instruments and blew on their pipes and horns, sometimes in solos, sometimes in ensemble with rhythmical drums. The populace enjoyed this from afar; they could not see the rituals going on inside the shrine, but they knew that the gods of other cities had come to pay homage and that the great king himself would "take the hand of Bel" to submit to his rule and get his oracles for the year ahead. The citizens, their houses crowded with country cousins, eagerly awaited the ninth day, when a great cortege would form and be visible as it slowly passed along the Sacred Way and out through the gate of Ishtar.

The Sacred Way, Procession Street, was straight and smooth, parallel to the river from the Ishtar Gate on the north and to Marduk's Temple on the south. It served as a thoroughfare for a royal and priestly enclave, walled and elevated from the huddled buildings of the old city. The military advantage of such a roadway justified its cost.

Though the Babylonian citizens did not participate in what was strictly a priestly ceremonial, they felt the excitement of spring, glimpsed bits of the opulent parade, ate, drank, and made merry. They knew that their great king was paying homage to their great god for the welfare of the empire, their peace, and prosperity. They needed this reassurance each year.

The pious Jewish exiles turned their backs to such heathen practices. As year after year habituated them to the excitement, some began to ask questions and even found amusement in the superstitions so lavishly displayed. Neziah was one of these.

On the ninth day of the spring festival he stayed at home and had cushions and stools placed on his jetty beyond the bordering date palms. To this viewing area he called his wife and household servants.

"Let's watch the fun," he said. "Quite a show, maybe the greatest on earth."

Lily demurred.

"Come on. What difference does it make?"

"Moses said no other gods ...."

"And the prophets say we are going back to Jerusalem."

"Of course. Yahweh is greater than Marduk."

"Well, we are far from him. He can't pollute you at this distance, my pious little Israelite. And how are you, returning to Judea from this world center, going to say you never saw any of the sights?"

Lily, not lacking curiosity, soon found her head craned and eyes popping at the distant spectacle as it appeared between tall buildings. First came the king, conqueror of the world, but humbled before his god, Marduk. His huge head of solid gold, his robes sparkling with jewels, riding in his golden chariot. He was followed by lesser gods, accompanied by their priests, bearing incense and making wild music in solemn beat and cadence.

"Spectacular!" "Oh, look at that crown!" "Oh, look at that robe!" "Did you ever see such a sight!" Exclamations went up from the Hanan wharf and from the other Jewish spectators lining the left bank of the Euphrates. The Babylonian laymen on their knees groaned and prayed. The fate of their nation depended on finding favor with Marduk for the coming year. Otherwise, war, flood, or famine would create chaos and ruin. At some point during the slow progress of the deity, the people knew that Marduk would ascend a tower and, on a golden bed, would consummate his marriage with a choice priestess. That mystic rite ensured fertility for all living things in the Land between the Rivers.

Lily, who had listened attentively to what Neziah told her about the fears of the people, said, "It is a great waste of substance and talent. How can they truly believe that a god made with human hands can create peace and prosperity or withhold them?"

"It is ridiculous. And that's not the end of the matter. They look into animal entrails to find omens."

"Disgusting."

"On the other hand, their wisest men go to the top of the ziggurat and study the heavens. They think the movements of the moon and stars foretell the future."

"That would be nice to know."

"Maybe so, maybe not."

"Let's get a Chaldean to foretell our future."

"They don't do it for people like us. They deal only in mighty affairs of state."

"It looks like ordinary people don't get much attention from their gods. What do they do?"

"Each family has its own personal god or gods of lesser quality. The people pay homage, bring offerings, and beg them to keep off evil spirits."

Lily laughed merrily. "They are too easily satisfied. All the same, I wish you'd hire a Chaldean to tell our future."

"I wouldn't believe him."

"I might—if he said we'd have a son."

Chapter 14
The Nile

Jarib was so confident and energetic when he left Jerusalem under siege that it never occurred to him that he could not join his family in Babylon in a year, or two, at most. Stealthily, but with assurance, he made his way out at agreed points, renewing his bribes to certain of Nebuchadnezzar's soldiery. The little black balls of poppy syrup had the desired results; Jarib was soon on the coast road to join his caravan, which was heading for the great markets in the Nile delta. There he would make his fortune.

He felt himself to be an experienced trader, having been in the business since he was big enough to beat a donkey. On the roads and in the markets of the fertile crescent, he had learned to buy low and sell high; to let his hand touch the profitable side of the scales; how to haggle and when to strike a bargain; and, most important of all, to work the dupes and avoid the crooks. Jarib, in his self-assurance, felt a glow of pride as he pictured his aristocratic father-in-law, the great precentor Jeduthun, and his submissive but cool wife, Lily, receiving from him rich gifts. He would make them comfortable even in Babylon, and they would gratefully admit that he was right in choosing to go down into Egypt. And he would have two sons, the start of a family, to comfort him in his old age.

Happily he arrived in the land of Goshen. Wasn't that where Moses broke the ancient heroes out of Pharaoh's bondage and led them into the Promised Land? That was a long time ago. A thousand years, and some. No matter; times had changed, but not human cupidity. Business was business.

But business proved to be poor, very poor that year. The war made men cautious. Worse was the competition: those rapacious Phoenicians, the wily Greeks, and other sailors from all over the eastern Mediterranean crowded into the Egyptian ports. Jarib's caravan broke up, each man going his separate way in search of better markets. After several days of vain attempts to trade to advantage, Jarib realized that he would have a hard time disposing of his wares at any price. He rightly suspected that his partners, those dear friends with whom he had laughed, eaten and done business, had taken advantage of his youth and unfamiliarity with Egyptian trade. The cloth they allotted him was too heavy, the jars too coarse. Nobody wanted such goods, and what they did want, he did not have. The Egyptians themselves made the finest textiles, the most exquisite vessels, the most gorgeous ornaments in the world. They were smart with numbers, too, measuring and calculating in their quick brains, while the Hebrew country boy was unloading his donkey.

Utterly discouraged, Jarib went back to his inn and ordered beer. Also sitting in the common room was an elderly man of mixed race, mostly Egyptian probably, who eyed young Jarib with fatherly concern. The two fell into conversation, and quickly agreed that business was very bad and not getting better.

"Your first time in Egypt, I take it," said the older man, who called himself Tibath.

Jarib had to admit that this was true, though he had carefully concealed the fact throughout this whole misadventure. He also admitted that he was in a hurry to make his fortune and rejoin his family in Babylon.

"Up river, that's the only place you have a chance to make good deals. Up river. That's where I came from, and that's where I'm going back," said Tibath. "Don't know why I ever came down here. I have a small boat, but I need help to row up against the stream. A strong back and arms when the wind fails, that's what I wait for."

Jarib considered a deal. Tibath, however, was firm about several matters. "It's just common sense. Your goods are too much for my prow. You can't sell that heavy stuff; the farther you go up the Nile, the hotter it gets."

Jarib said, "I thank you for your good advice, kind sir. I guess land travel is the only way for me."

Tibath laughed, "My dear boy, you will never get to Thebes by land. Too many walls and ditches in the cultivated fields along the river. And east and west of that ribbon of green, there is nothing but sand, shifting sand. It will eat you up—if robbers don't get you first."

Jarib groaned.

In the end, he dumped his unsaleable wares, sold his beasts, bought beads and trinkets, and rowed Tibath's boat out of the mouth of the Nile toward ancient Memphis. They passed the pyramids. They admired the skill that built such structures. The older man thought aloud of the folly of spending your life on a tomb, only to have it broken into by a clever thief.

"People never learn anything," he said. "The pharaohs kept on doing it. There's a great underground graveyard across the river from Thebes. You can't see it, but grave robbers have been looting it for years. I'm told there is not much left except the painted walls—if you can find them."

Jarib considered finding an intact royal burial as a possible source of his fortune.

"Forget it, Jarib. All the valuables were taken long before your grandfather was born. There's nothing there but rocks and sand. Nothing. You'll see."

They sailed past Karnak. Jarib gawked at the towering columns, carved and closely clustered.

"That's where the priests and the king worship Ammon. This is as close as you can get."

"But the People? Where do they worship their god?"

"Well, the sun shines all day, doesn't it? We can feel how powerful its rays are, even if it makes us afraid when it sinks at night. Then there are plenty of lesser gods for about everything you can think of. You pick out one that fits your needs. Very convenient."

Jarib suppressed a snort of contempt. They were drawing in at Thebes. Across the wide river, the kings of old had dug their final resting places. Tibath was right. He'd never find his fortune in that wasteland.

Tibath decided to pull in and rest a couple of days. They found a juncture of canal and river, paid for docking space, and sought an inn. Jarib enjoyed a wash down, a good soup, and a comfortable bed while Tibath engaged in earnest conversation with some cronies. As they spoke pure Egyptian instead of the lingua franca of traders, Jarib could not understand what they said. He wasn't interested anyway, relying on the older man to pass on the best advice.

So he did: better commerce lay farther up the Nile, the very best being beyond the second cataract. There were big fortunes to be made in deals with the blacks, who brought in gold, ivory, curious animals and aromatic woods in exchange for beads and baubles. That rich prospect lent strength to Jarib's muscles so that he rowed and poled, when he had to, back and forth, farther and farther south. Tibath swapped melons and such for grain and vegetables, first on one side of the broad river and then on the other. Jarib asked his friend why he engaged in such petty commerce when great treasures lay ahead. Tibath said he was too old for that sort of thing. Landing by a neat, luxuriant patch cultivated by a peasant and his family, Jarib saw that their simple mud hut had no roof. Again in midstream he asked about it.

"That man is evidently prosperous and flourishing. Why does he live in such a shack with no roof?"

"Because it never rains in these parts. When the river is in flood it washes away everything. That's bad. But the good thing is that it leaves much silt to give life to the land. Then the farmer has to have his field measured again. And he has to work from sun up to sun down to take advantage of the growing season. He doesn't have time to loll around in a house, and he doesn't need a roof."

Jarib allowed that it was all very different in Judea.

In their zigzag progress south, they passed handsome temples and gigantic statues of long-dead kings. One day they could go no farther, for they were stopped by forts on either side of the Nile. Cataracts lay ahead to halt river traffic even if the military had not.

Tibath went ashore to report. He brought back a stout fellow whom he introduced to Jarib as one who could lead him to the trading post in the interior. Jarib thanked his mentor and docilely followed his new leader. But not

Exile

to fame and fortune. When Jarib looked back over the years, it was hard for him to believe that he had been so easily duped.

The "trading center" turned out to be a collection of men, mostly Jews, who lived separately in the forest with their black wives and children. They swapped trade goods with black men bringing elephant tusks, aromatic woods, and sometimes gold from the jungle. Periodically the white men brought their wares to a fixed place, where Egyptian traders took what they wanted and paid poorly in return. The whole operation was supervised by overseers with armed guards. The Jews were in fact prisoners. They could not escape through savages and mountains to the south, east, and west, nor would the Egyptians let them leave by river to the north.

For a while Jarib made the best of the situation. He made love with his seductive wives and let them do the work. It was their relatives who brought in the wood and animals wanted by the Egyptians. But he saw no gold. And the heat was suffocating. The insects and snakes intolerable. He drank more beer and somehow obtained more wives. The more wives he had, the more trouble. They made more beer and brought in more trading tribesmen. In a lucid moment he counted seven wives, the perfect number. He disliked them. He hated the place. He hated the Egyptians, who had lured him into this place. He cursed his erstwhile partners in trade. They had cheated him. Everybody took advantage of him. He would get even, beat them at their lies and tricks!

He watched and waited with a mask of sleepy indifference, but behind the mask was his sharp, calculating brain. The wiles Jarib had developed in trade grew into a low cunning: watch for the slightest advantage, seize it, and shake it to pieces, no matter what the other fellow did or thought. There had to be a goal. No doubt about that: He must escape from this filthy, bug infested country and go home. He must find an advantage.

Jarib's seven wives lived in separate kraals, spaced in a circle. It was the wisdom of the race that no two women can live in peace under one roof. Each had her own garden plot and some goats. Jarib visited each in turn to eat, drink, and ease his loins. There were children, of course. Wife number Three, whose hut was next to that of wife number One, seemed to be the only female who did not drop a baby every year. Jarib found that convenient and rather favored number Three, a cause for jealousy and some fighting.

The roar that broke out one fine morning was so loud that you could hear the yelling and screeching out to the water hole. The thump of smashing pots brought Jarib to the scene. He could not understand a word the women screamed, but he instantly understood the cause of their fury.

Number Three had found beside the trail an old woman abandoned by slave traders. Having no children or parent to pet, number Three brought the poor creature home and took care of her until she regained strength, and with strength, usefulness. The old woman became number Three's slave. It amused Jarib to hear his wife ordering her about, all the while secreting her within her kraal.

Now number One had discovered the situation and pulled rank: number Three had no right to a servant; she would have her, for she was number One!

Jarib's entrance stopped the fight, but not the words. He settled the dispute by taking the older woman home with him. He called her Zelzah, for he discovered that she was indeed "shade in the heat."

Chapter 15
Jarib

The party from the interior arrived at the first cataract tired, sweaty, but excited. Six women were dragging a sort of sledge. A seventh was bent double under a load of skins. Jarib strode ahead. An Egyptian ran up to him and, pounding the earth with a stave, said, "unload here."

Though the language barrier was still serious even after a decade in the wilds of upper Egypt, Jarib got the message and gestured to his wives that they could put down their burdens. They ran chattering and laughing toward the spot where a great Egyptian boat was disgorging trade goods below the rough water. They fingered this, grabbed that; and finally, one by one, they came back to Jarib's spot, carrying bags of beads and baskets of trinkets they had selected for themselves. Zelzah brought back lengths of cloth and a long papyrus rope. Jarib sighed in resignation. From previous experience, he knew that again he would barely break even.

An Egyptian merchant came up and examined the sledge. The great mahogany tree trunk was common; the ivory tusks were old and broken; the skins were mangy. Jarib disagreed, loudly pointing out the beauty and desirable qualities of his wares. The Egyptian passed on. He saw the monkey, the pet of wife number Six. He said he'd take that. Loud protest came from its owner. In the end the Egyptian took everything in exchange for what the women had seized. It was a deal, and Jarib was free to go back to the jungle and start over again.

But this time it was different, and Zelzah, the Ethiopian slave, made the difference. Jarib had found in this woman a treasure. She had nursed him through the ague, using herbs and leaves from the forest; she kept his hut clean, fed him lean meat instead of fat, and climbed trees to find eggs, fruits, and tough vines. She was small of bone and feature, unlike the native of Nubia, and she spoke a little Hebrew, learned from the old people of her land, which lay far to the east. Like Jarib, she wanted to go home.

Less beer and more jungle craft were the starters. Jarib began to climb and swing. These skills were hampered by dizziness, and so Jarib left off the brew. He learned to walk without making a sound and to lie quietly hidden in ambush. Zelzah taught him to observe the habits of the birds and beasts. They stole far into the jungle to the water hole, where the great carnivores drank. They watched lions and tigers stalk their prey, the old and weak, or the young and foolish of the grazing herds. Jarib began to have admiration and respect for the strong beasts and for the cunning Nubians, who caught them in their aged weakness and hastened their death.

The strong killed the weak and lived. The less strong picked the carcass and survived. That was the law of the jungle. Follow it or perish. Jarib absorbed this. It was different from the law of Moses, which his parents had taught him to recite, but as everybody knew, the law of Moses did not apply to business. And Jarib was in business. Was not his escape the weightiest business?

It started with a false grin. Jarib, who had once tolerated the overseer in surly silence, now welcomed him with hospitality.

"Come in, gentlemen. Come in! Zelzah, bring our guests some beer."

The overseer and his two guards sat down on the earthen bench that ringed the circular hut. They drank. They deigned to eat some boiled zebra. They drank again. The two guards fell asleep. The overseer continued to talk, mostly boasting of the widespread power of Egypt.

"You have traveled to the regions east of the great river?"

"No, but I've heard about it."

"High mountains there?"

The overseer nodded and went into details that Jarib, because of his limited knowledge of the language, could not understand. It was the same with Zelzah, who had come from that land. Try as Jarib might, he could never get the specific information he needed to find a route to the Red Sea.

On subsequent inspections there was more or less the same sequence but with easier manners. Under his hypocritical smile, Jarib hated his bosses more and more. The arrogant knaves! But he had to have a weapon.

Wife number One's father entered, carrying a fine spear, a stone wedge lashed to an ebony pole.

Jarib made swapping motions and offered a basket of beads. The big black man spat contemptuously and stalked away. Jarib hated the blacks with increasing fury. He hated the heat. He hated the insects—and the snakes and the leeches. His skin was a mass of bites. He hated himself.

Seasons passed, Jarib knew, but he could not tell when or how many. It was always the same: monotony of luxuriant foliage, monotony of rain, monotony of bugs, monotony of people who enjoyed monotony.

"Hi, boss," Jarib jovially greeted the overseer and guards.

"We're hot and ready for cool beer," was the response.

The men ate and drank, and drank and ate. They stretched out on the curved bench.

" You want a woman now, I guess," said Jarib.

"Yeah, bring 'em on."

"I'll take you over to number Four tonight."

Exile

En route, the overseer stepped out into the bushes to answer the call of nature.

Snap! Thump!

The overseer went sprawling over a cord stretched under the leaves and hit the ground. Jarib was on him in a flash, pounding his head with a rock. He took his bronze dagger. He put a noose around his neck. Then he and Zelzah tugged at the loose end of the rope, and the overseer was twisting high in the leaf canopy, his neck and windpipe broken. A very quiet execution.

Jarib then led Zelzah back into his hut to get the two snoring guards. With the dagger, Jarib made short work of them. He took their knives and spears and gave the dead bodies a few extra thrusts.

Zelzah brought out a bundle and a basket. "We must leave now. Quickly!"

"No. You stay here and tell everybody I'm sick. I'll hide and come back for you later."

He grabbed the basket and fled. He had no intention of returning. Zelzah had served his purpose to the limit of her usefulness.

From her, he took the general direction of his journey: southeast. From her, he had learned that there was gold in the mountains and that the hated Egyptians used Ethiopian slave labor to mine and process the ore. From her, he heard that the native ruler of Ethiopia considered himself descended from Solomon and the Queen of Sheba and was therefore, sympathetic to Hebrews, especially Judeans. That was the route to fortune and the way home.

Through increasingly rough and barren terrain Jarib followed a stream. He came to a dead end at a sheer cliff and had to turn back. This was the first, but not the last time. Food became a real problem. The land looked like a waste heap, God's dumping ground when He made the good earth. That was the trouble with God; He never could make things come out right. Jarib hated God. He cursed Him when he had to kill a man for the food he carried. He got used to killing. He lost count of the wayfarers and the wrong turns. Long years after he had started his journey he finally saw the waters of the sea ahead. From north to south, it stretched its welcoming arms. Could this be the Red Sea? It was more like green. Was this the sea that parted itself long enough for Moses to lead his ancestors across and then inundated the pursuing hosts of Pharaoh? A likely story, about as useful as the law of Moses.

Jarib saw a fishing boat trawling slowly in his direction. He waited.

Two years later he was again waiting, at that very spot. Waiting on the quaff at Dilbat for the boat to Babylon. On the dock that day was another, much younger man.

Though strangers, they were suffering the common inconveniences of travel and so fell into conversation. They agreed that the heat was intolerable, that there was no excuse for the delay in passenger service to the metropolis.

The younger, whose open, smiling face had never looked on guile or hostility in his whole experience, affably continued, "Surely it will pull in before dark. I must get back home. Should have been there today. My wife is expecting me."

The older said, "My feet are killing me. Come, let's put our feet in the water, cool 'em off."

The younger said, "Good idea," took off his well-made sandals and looked with pity on the twisted, swollen feet of his new acquaintance.

The older man grumbled, "They don't make good sandals anymore. These are from Basra. God knows where before that."

The younger said, "I am a shoemaker. I never saw any like these. You have traveled far?"

"Too far for old feet, as you see. Perhaps your wife would like a gold bracelet to soothe her anger at your late arrival?" He pulled a little gold band out of his girdle. It was a pretty thing, set with blue stone.

"Oh, she's never angry with me, but I'd like to give her a present. Let me see it."

"You can pay?"

"Yes, of course. I am well rewarded for my services." The younger man reached within his clothing and pulled out a pouch, which hung from his neck on a thong. He saw that the older man was needy and offered him more than the bracelet was worth. A moment or two of bargaining and the deal was struck.

The sun sank below the horizon. The older man rose to his gnarled feet. No boat in sight. Then, like a flash, he planted his dagger in the younger man's back, stripped him, and pushed him into the Euphrates.

There was a leather case left at the end of the dock. Jarib opened it and in the twilight was a lyre of delicate workmanship and costly decoration. He was tempted. No. Such an instrument would be traced. He hurled it far out into the river.

Chapter 16
The Lyre

When Jeduthun first came to Nippur at the special invitation of the leaders of the Jewish community, he was greeted and honored with the respect he had earned in the Temple of Jerusalem and more lately in Babylon. His glorious voice, his acute ear, and his perfect memory made him preeminent among the musicians of the time. He was kept busy writing down all the songs of praise he remembered from his youth, as well as others which he had composed. He trained two choirs, one of singing men, another of singing women, and he taught them well in the proper rendition of the melodies. He trained musicians, those who played on stringed instruments, or blew the reeds and pipes, or struck the drums and cymbals. He even helped the craftsmen who made the instruments, letting them use as models his own precious collection brought in a chest on that long journey into exile. He was called on for solo performances. He was a happy man, his talents fully engaged with a noble purpose.

The elders of Judah, who had honored him on his arrival in Nippur and shared their mission of recording the heritage of the Jewish people, one by one came to the limits of life. Jeduthun found himself more and more engaged in funeral music and less and less in the active work of the scribes. Younger men with different ideas took over. They were not interested in what he had to offer but were very excited about the latest prophet, a second Isaiah who had fresh answers to old problems and a firm prediction that their captivity would be ended by Cyrus, a great conqueror from the east.

Jeduthun found an old prophet from the days of Josiah, Habukkuk, and set some of his splendid poetry to music:

> *"What profiteth the carven image that its maker hath engraved it; the mettled image and a teacher of lies, that the maker of his work trusteth in it, to make dumb idols?*
>
> *Woe to him that sayeth to the wood, Awake; to the dumb stone, Arise, it shall teach! Behold, it is laid over with gold and silver, and there is no breath in the midst of it.*
>
> *But the Lord is in His holy temple; let all the earth keep silence before Him."*[19]

The young priest-scribes thanked old Jeduthun politely, but he could see that they thought him and his music antiquated. They were completely taken up with arguing about the full meaning of the new messenger, who brought new life and hope to their exile.

> "Remember these, O Jacob and Israel; for thou art My servant: I have formed thee; thou art My servant: O Israel, thou shalt not be forgotten by Me.
> I have blotted out, like a thick cloud, thy transgressions, and like a cloud thy sins: return unto Me; for I have redeemed thee.
> Sing, O ye heavens; for the Lord hath done it: shout, ye lower parts of the earth: break forth into singing, ye mountains, O forest, and every tree therein: for the Lord hath redeemed Jacob, and glorified Himself in Israel.
> Thus saith the Lord, thy redeemer, and He that formed thee from the womb: I am the Lord who maketh all things; that stretcheth forth the heavens alone; who spreadeth abroad the earth by Myself.
> Who frustrateth the tokens of the liars, and maketh diviners mad; who turneth wise men backward, and maketh their knowledge foolish;
> Who confirmeth the word of His servant, and performeth the counsel of His messengers; who saith to Jerusalem, thou shalt be inhabited; and to the cities of Judah, ye shall be built, and I will raise up the decayed places thereof;
> Who with to the deep, be dry, and I will dry up thy rivers;
> Who saith of Cyrus, he is my shepherd, and shall perform all my pleasure: even saying to Jerusalem, thou shalt be built; and to the temple, thy foundation shall be laid."[20]

This was heavy stuff, and there was more: the suffering servant. What manner of savior was he? The new prophet visioned the nation as the redeemer of the world. Many agreed that the Chosen People had experienced a history of agony for their sins of the world. Others thought that a Messiah would come from the root of Jesse, as promised in the covenant with David. The young men had advanced far beyond their elders and had not patience with them.

Jeduthun wanted to enter into these deliberations but he could not hear clearly all that was said. They spoke so fast and so low. Perhaps his remarks were off the mark? Perhaps they thought he was senile? They acted like it. And so Jeduthun kept silent and remained at home. He found it hard to pass the time alone in his room. There were left a few of his contemporaries who would drop in. He was glad to see them come, but gladder to see them go, for the telling of their aches and pains increased his own.

He would compose a song and write it down. His eyesight was so dim that he could no longer read, much less write all the jots and tittles of his language. So, he sat and remembered songs and legends of old. He recalled a bit of lore not generally known. It would be a reason for visiting the writing house and talking with the scribes.

The scribe at work was also a priest and very busy. He looked up from a scroll. Jeduthun did not know him. He introduced himself. The name meant nothing to the young scribe, who did not even lay down his quill.

"Yes?"

Jeduthun persevered. "I have a story from the beginning of our ancestors, even the son of ...."

"His name?"

"Cain. His son was..."

"What did this fellow do that we should put him in the scroll of origins?"

"He, Jubal Cain, invented musical instruments."

"Oh, that. We have that. Didn't you tell us that last year? He was the father of all who handle the harp and pipe."

Jeduthun said he was sorry to have interrupted, tried to hide his mortification, and returned to his lonely room. The old crone who boarded him brought food. He barely touched it.

He came down with an illness that kept him in bed for several weeks. When he returned to his choir, a new director motioned him to the back row. Thus it was made plain to the once illustrious maestro that he was no longer needed or wanted.

Jeduthun had to admit to himself that he was alone, frightfully alone, with no ties to bind him or to support him. He was empty, waiting for the final gust that would topple him into Sheol. His family....Those were the good old times when they were together, sharing the hardships of the journey to Babylon and the joys of watching Ethan grow up. That adorable, fat boy who would take his stance, wait for Grandfather to play an elaborate introduction, and then burst forth in song as the most polished virtuoso, like his grandfather. And then there was Lily, whose whole interest in life was to take care of them. A mere woman, of course, and therefore not to be judged too harshly when she wanted a man in her bed. Jarib had been gone years. She did have the good sense to sin with Neziah, a son worthy of his illustrious father. He could forgive them, but could they forgive him after his harsh judgment? No use to open himself to further blows.

But he would summon Ethan again.

He had repeatedly sent word up river to Ethan that he wanted to see him. There was always an affectionate reply to the effect that Ethan thought often and lovingly of his dear grandfather but that he could not leave his engagements that season. He would try to get to Nippur as soon as possible. Jeduthun, of course, understood. Ethan was now the paramount musician in Babylonia. He went about to the different Jewish communities to sing and to teach. Furthermore, he had composed a master piece of a penitential psalm by which, through God's grace, he had wrought a complete recovery from his dying wife. Jeduthun chuckled to himself. He surely would like to see that boy, with his shining face and voice, now grown to full beard and fame. It would be rewarding to see his own blood, his own pupil, showing the results of childhood training. The famous man would thank him and invite him back to their old home. It was a dear dream.

Meanwhile, Jeduthun thought of some truths that he wanted to share with Ethan and all these brash, young people. He would make another psalm, a farewell prayer to be remembered in the human condition. It would be what Moses would have said as he looked afar at the Promised Land he would never enter, the prayer he would have made for his sinning, wandering people after forty years in the wilderness.

"*O Lord, thou hast been our dwelling place in all generations....*"

There was a knock, and an old bore entered. He said he came to inquire about Jeduthun s health, but he really came because he had nothing else to do except complain about his swollen joints and the wretched food they both had to put up with in their wretched boarding house.

Jeduthun knew better than to answer the inquiry about his health. Nor did it matter that he only nodded absently to his visitor's monologue. "In all generations...." He tried to catch the thread that had been broken.

There came another knock.

"Grandfather!" It was Ethan's voice.

"Ethan!" was the joyous welcoming reply.

The two poets embraced.

The old visitor lingered long enough to be introduced and then tactfully withdrew. He now could visit other people with a choice morsel of news: he had met the famous tenor Ethan and found him quite charming. Others, not so fortunate, would welcome the bearer of such news and give him opportunity to elaborate on it.

Ethan sat beside his grandfather and took his hand in his.

"How are you doing, Grandfather?"

"Fine," said the old man. It was his stock answer. Ethan chose to accept it.

"It is good to see you looking so well and surrounded by friends in this quiet place." Ethan patted the old man's hand and looked earnestly into his dim eyes. "We think of you all the time and I've been on the point of coming to see you many times but always something comes up that I must attend to. You see...."

Exile

Ethan launched into an account of his activities, all important, all involving other important people. These names were strange to Jeduthun, who understood that they were the new generation of the rich and powerful in Babylon, an odd mix of Jews and natives.

"How is Sebot?" Jeduthun asked about an old family friend.

"I don't see him these days, but I'll tell him you asked."

And Ethan continued his discourse, of which he was the main subject. Even the news that Nebuchadnezzar had gone crazy and was eating grass on all fours in the desert was turned to Ethan as his opportunity for further important engagements.

"You see, when the Marduk priests could not celebrate the New Year without the king, we musiciains organized festivities. I must say that we put on magnificent processions with full orchestras and great choruses. I wrote all of the new music and led it and sang lead in most of the old."

"Did you use Mushi?" Mushi was a valuable member of Jeduthun's choir at Eleazar's house.

Ethan paused and thought a second. "I think I heard that Mushi died last year."

Jeduthun inquired about the family, and Ethan warmed to that subject. His boys had grown up with minds of their own, brilliant and handsome. They had many friends in high places. "Shama is frequently at court, invited by his friend Daniel. He says the parties are very sumptuous ...."

Jeduthun exclaimed in dismay.

"Oh, Grandfather, times are changing and we have to keep up. It's a hectic pace, all right. You ought to come see what's going on in Babylon. You wouldn't know the place.

"But I must be going. I'm on my way to Dilbat to try to enroll Sabta in their school of star studies. The boy is determined to study the heavenly bodies, won't hear of marriage. I have a Babylonian friend in charge of the Dilbat Ziggurat, and I'm going to ask him to take Sabta as a pupil in that observatory."

"Ethan, don't be in such a hurry to leave. I am writing a psalm for you. I will give you the words and you can compose suitable music. Tarry a bit and listen."

"Sorry, dear Grandfather. I must be on my way. Naarah expected me at home yesterday but I decided to come by here. She will worry. You can send your poem by messenger, and I'll try to find time to think of a tune."

Suddenly the old man was struck by the possibility that he might never again see Ethan, the center of his hopes and dreams.

"Wait," he said, rising to his feet. He hobbled across the room and took from its central place on a shelf an antique lyre of exquisite workmanship.

"I give you this, my son. It has been called David's harp. At any rate, it is very old and very sweet. Enjoy...."

"O Grandfather, you shouldn't," murmured Ethan, eagerly taking the instrument. He found its case and put it in.

The two men clasped each other in farewell. The younger strode off toward the canal. The older put his head on the table and wept.

By next morning Jeduthun had pulled himself together and resolved to get on with his life. He was glad that his grandson, really a son to him, was so talented and famous that he had no time for him. It would be sad if it were otherwise. And the great grandchildren. How much time had he devoted to his grandparents? Precious little, of course. Best not to be a burden. Better get on with the Moses psalm.

He concentrated until interrupted by his landlady. She wanted his opinion on which piece of cloth to buy. Jeduthun, who at this stage of visual impairment could not tell red from green, listened until she had persuaded herself to select her original choice. But she did not go. She launched into her favorite subject—food—and there was no stopping her. Jeduthun's thoughts turned to his poem and stayed there until she finally left.

"Another thing I must remember: Don't talk so much. I don't want to hasten the end of my friends by boring them to death."

He gave a chuckle as he wondered whether he bored God. And he heard a peal of thunder in the distance like a gigantic laugh.

The poem was finished and written large and wide, spaced on his few remaining sheets of papyrus. He had made a splendid melody for it, too, and indicated voice tones by marks above the words. They were marks like the gestures he would make in directing the choir. That was a good idea—if he could find a scribe capable of copying his crude manuscript. He marked off the accents. He hummed it over and found it good.

"Lord, Thou hast been our dwelling place in all generations. Before the mountains were brought forth, or even Thou hadst formed the earth and the world, even from everlasting to everlasting, Thou art God.

Thou turnest man to destruction; and sayest, Return, ye children of men.

For a thousand years in Thy sight are but as yesterday when it is past, and as a watch in the night.

Thou carriest them away as with a flood; they are like asleep: in the morning they are like grass which groweth up.

It flourisheth and groweth up; in the evening it is cut down, and withereth.

For we are consumed by Thine anger, and by Thy wrath we are troubled.

Thou hast set our iniquities before Thee, our secret sins in the light of Thy countenance.

For all our days are passed away in Thy wrath: we spend our years as a tale that is told.

> *The days of our years are threescore years and ten; and if by reason of strength they be foreseore years, yet is their strength labour and sorrow; for it is soon cut off and we fly away.*
>
> *Who knoweth the power of Thine anger? Even according to Thy fear, so is Thy wrath."*
>
> *So teach us to number our days, that we may apply our hearts unto wisdom.*
>
> *Return, O Lord, how long? And let it repent Thee concerning Thy servants.*
>
> *O, satisfy us early with Thy mercy; that we may rejoice and be glad all our days.*
>
> *Make us glad according to the days wherein thou has afflicted us, and the years wherein we have seen evil.*
>
> *Let thy work appear unto Thy servants, and Thy glory unto their children.*
>
> *And let the beauty of the Lord our God be upon us and establish Thou the work of our hands upon us; yea, the work of our hands establish Thou it."*[21]

It was another long day for Jeduthun. He found it difficult to "kill time," as the saying goes. There was so much of it, now that he had no occupation. He'd be glad for night to come when lack of vision, deafness, and weak knees would make no difference. He could then thank his maker for having brought him safely through.

There was a knock on the door, which the old man welcomed with glad surprise.

"Come in! Come in!" he cried.

He did not recognize the stranger, but his name ....

"I am Jarib, your son."

"Of course, of course. Welcome, welcome. You and Lily ...yes, yes. You went down into Egypt—and were long gone."

The two men were genuinely glad to see each other and fell into each other's arms.

"Come, sit beside me and tell me all about it. This side is better ...."

Jarib had no intention of telling anybody "all about it," and he soon saw that what he did tell was unintelligible to Jeduthun. Coming out of Egypt by way of the land of "burnt faces" was to the deaf old man the "burnt places" of Judea. He wept in sympathy. Jarib was touched. Impulsively he drew a leather sack from his girdle.

"But it was not entirely without profit. I have brought you a gift."

Jeduthun took the bag and, without opening it, tossed it on the table. Jarib continued with an account of his having sought the family in Babylon and of being told of Jeduthun's residence in Nippur.

"It seems that Ethan was away on a long journey."

"Ethan! Yes, you should be very proud of Ethan, a great musician with many engagements and many important friends."

"And Lily?"

"Oh, my boy. I am sorry to have to tell you that after so many years of waiting, she took another husband."

Jarib clenched his jaws. "She should have waited. She can't expect me to take her back."

"Do not be so hard on the poor girl. I was very harsh to her at the time, driving her from the house. Now I wish…."

"You did not stone her, according to the law? It must have been a clear case of adultery."

"But you were gone such a very long time, Jarib. And poor, weak women need husbands. Even Lily has that weakness. I dare say you were not entirely without women to ease your loins in Egypt. No?"

Jarib admitted with a snarl that this was so. "But with men it's different. No law, no punishment for us."

"Well, perhaps there should be. But let's talk about Ethan. He will be a real son to you—so handsome, so talented. He has two fine sons, fine young fellows whom he is trying to get started in life. One wants to study the stars in the observatory in Dilbat. Imagine that, quite like a Chaldean. Ethan came by here to see me not too long ago. He was on his way…."

At the mention of Dilbat, Jarib started to fidget.

I gave Ethan my treasure of a lyre. The one I brought from the Temple…."

Jarib rushed from the room.

Jeduthun thought, "I must have wearied him," and opened the bag, the gift of Jarib. He was astonished and grateful that his son-in-law thought so much of him. There were rings, chains, pins, and a pretty bracelet set with a blue stone.

"Just the thing for Lily," he pictured to himself. Yes, with this gift, he'd go back to Babylon to see his family. Just a short visit. He didn't want to be a burden. He'd give presents and return. Yes, he could hire a scribe and do some serious work.

He smiled as he imagined his loving reunion with Lily and Ethan. Their children…He felt drowsy and put his head down on the table.

That night death came and carried him home, the smile still on his lips.

That night Jarib, too, finished his journey. He hanged himself.

---

[19] Habakkuk 2
[20] Isaiah 44
[21] Psalms 90

Chapter 17
The Widow

Time touched lightly the House of Hanan, but inevitably it did its work of change—more here, less there, erosion of the surface revealing the essential core. Riches piled upon riches in the market house while the people involved lost strength. Help was hired and fired by reason of theft. More bookkeepers were needed. Neziah found himself working longer hours while Lily protested that he was killing himself. She suggested that he bring back one of his sons to help in Babylon.

"That won't help," said Neziah. "Both boys are fully engaged handling their own operations. If one is called here, the other will be jealous. Besides, young men know it all, consider older men fools. They want to take charge. My dear wife, I am too old to be bossed by a young cock of the walk."

"Not old, my love. But you must take care of yourself."

Neziah consented to having a couch brought into his cubicle of an office. He would lie down for a nap in the heat of the day.

Lily became more and more interested in the management of the home estate on the west bank of the river. The gardens and orchards bloomed and fruited; the flocks increased the production of meat and wool; the looms and spindles and fishing boats brought in a surplus. All knew the watchful eye and careful planning of the lady of the house. She was becoming the ideal wife described by King Solomon, and she was proud to report to the master, when he came home late and tired, that his home estate was not only self-sustaining but showing a profit.

They both laughed privately at the change in their steward, Bunah. He grew thin and waspish, said he needed help and got it. Then he sat down and issued orders. Next he got up and scolded. The helpers were slow and slovenly. Bunah made the serving of meals an ordeal by his insistence on precise service: "Place it here. Here! Be careful! Place it. Don't slosh. Careful!"

Lily's maid Adah, on the other hand, grew fat and dumpy. She brought a young girl to help her with the heavy work of massaging the mistress while she confined herself to the more delicate tasks of painting and braiding. Oftener than not, the young girl left in tears, threatening not to come back. When she did not return, another was found, and it was the same story over again.

Gomer, Neziah's body servant, took full charge of his master; he no longer took orders, he gave them. Neziah just smiled indulgently.

To Lily he said, "I guess as we grow older we grow crankier."

"More like ourselves?" she suggested.

"Crankier. More set in our ways. Others, likewise obstinate and perverse, call it cranky."

"Tell me, O wise and loving husband, why is it so easy to find our faults in others and so hard to see them in ourselves?"

"Lack of love, my love. I see no fault in you. Let us make love."

Neziah was not surprised when one dismal, rainy evening Gomer handed him a cup and said, "Drink this and enjoy the night:" He drank, and the drinking of the aphrodisiac became a habit.

Adah, painting her mistress's nipples, murmured, "I have procured for you and the master a very precious elixir." She put her lips to Lily's ear and whispered, "A love potion." Then she resumed her painting and went on murmuring. "You will find that it enhances your pleasures in bed. Not that you need it, of course, but you might try it."

That, too, became a habit. Neziah took a potion at the hands of Gomer while he dressed for dinner. The couple drank Adah's brew as they undressed. One night as they sat at the table, Lily noted the whitening of her husband's temples for the first time. He was such a distinguished looking man, perhaps a bit pale and unusually silent.

"Do you not feel well, my dear?"

"No, no, it's nothing. A pain. I've had it before. It will pass. Not bad; maybe indigestion."

They finished the meal, of which Neziah ate practically nothing, and went into their bedroom. The household settled down for the night.

Suddenly, there was a scream. Servants rushed to the big chamber. They found Lily holding Neziah head in her lap. "Doctors! Bring doctors! Fast!"

When the doctors arrived, they pronounced Neziah dead. Lily refused to believe it. They tried everything they knew in vain. They made Lily drink poppy juice.

Bunah took over. He knew how funerals were handled in the best families.

Lily sat stony faced and dry eyed in a corner. The seamstress made her a garment of the finest sackcloth available. Adah dressed her in it and powdered her hair with a fine sprinkling of ashes. She could not bring herself to think of the corpse.

"Send for the sons of this house."

"They have been sent for, my lady."

Waiting became intolerable as the days passed. Neziah's body had been strapped in linen winding cloth filled with spices and carried to the coolest courtyard of the house. Friends came to offer condolences. Lily kept to her room. She tried to remember happier days when she first enjoyed that room.

Yes, the first "anniversary" when he gave her that rope of big pearls. She went to her jewel chest, put the pearls around her neck and clutched them to her heart.

Bunah stood before her and said, "My lady, we must have the burial. The body begins to ...."

She spared him further embarrassment saying, "Yes, I know. The heat. Yes, tomorrow. Go ahead."

On the morrow she pulled herself together and was starting from her room when she remembered the pearls. "Not suitable," she thought and put them in the pouch-pocket made into a seam of her dress. She noticed that her fingers were still heavy with rings. She slipped them off and put them, too, into the pocket and forgot them as she walked steadily behind her husband's bier to the landing. Seated in the boat, she put a veil over her face and spoke to no one.

The next day the elder son, Azaz, came from Elam. He roared at her with indignation for having buried his father without him. His wife required the services of Adah after such a hurried journey. Lily said nothing, but her heart cried out:

"Neziah, where are you? Speak to this angry man. I am helpless without you."

Temen, the second son, arrived a day later and was furious with both his stepmother and his brother. They should have waited for him, allowed for the distance and the pressure of business in Damascus. It was apparent that he had no intention of deferring to an elder brother's claim on the estate.

The row raged on both banks of the Euphrates. Scribes (both Jewish and Babylonian) representing each side took inventory: so much in the warehouse came from the east, so much from the west, so much in doubt. Angry charges and counter charges rent the air of the entrepot and its environs. They were continued in the home compound when the brothers returned for the night.

Their wives squabbled over the contents of the house, each snatching at what she wanted only to be yelled at by the other with reasons why she should not have it. They invaded Lily's quarters. They took her clothes, her jewels, her cosmetics, her mirror, the rug from the floor and the cushions from the bed. Lily sat in silence, the veil over her face.

She tried to think of pleasant times but could find none, such was her grief at loosing Neziah. The things did not matter, nor the indignity of her treatment. From the utter emptiness that followed the loss of her reason for living, she found no words of protest, only sighs and furtive tears. He was gone. Where? She was alone. Why? She was afraid. Of what?!

She comforted herself for a moment with the remembrance of David's immortal song of faith. It was hard to put herself in the place of a sheep but worth the try.

> *"The Lord is my shepherd, I shall not want.*
> *He maketh me to lie down in green pastures: He leadeth me beside the still waters.*
> *He restoreth my soul. He leadeth me in the paths of righteousness for His name's sake.*
> *Yea, though I walk through the valley of the shadow of death, I will fear no evil: for Thou art with me. Thy rod and Thy staff they comfort me.*
> *Thou preparest a table before me in the presence of mine enemies; Thou anointest my head with oil; my cup runneth over.*
> *Surely goodness and mercy shall follow me all the days of my life; and I shall dwell in the house of the Lord forever."* [22]

The widow sighed, waiting for a voice that did not answer. She repeated the psalm. She kept on repeating it, sometimes silently, sometimes audibly. The hard-hearted said she had lost her mind.

The sons of Neziah disagreed on all things except one: Lily must go. There was no argument about that; she was an outsider, an interloper, and a nuisance.

Bunah was summoned and ordered to return the wretched woman to where she belonged, the other side of the river, right away.

"Yes, sirs. I shall take her as soon as she can be ready."

"No, not you. You have duties here. Get a couple of boatmen. No. One will be enough. She won't have any baggage. She is to take only the clothes on her back."

So it was that Lily found herself standing in a pile of rubble on the east bank of the Euphrates within walking distance of the home which she had shared with her father and her son.

Both had thrust her out with harsh words. She could not go there. She would not let them hurt her again. She was quivering from rejection and judgment and could not stand another blow. She sat down in the street. And under her veil she wept.

---

[22] Psalms 23

Chapter 18
The Loom

The house, bigger than most, but in a sad state of disrepair, stood at a turn in the winding street. Lily had been eyeing it since first light and had seen no one enter or leave. Perhaps it was empty. At dusk she knocked at the door. To her surprise, it was promptly opened by a drab old woman, also in sackcloth.

"Oh, you poor thing. Come in. Do come in."

Lily, sensing the sympathy she needed, stumbled in and said, "I am the widow Mahalia."

She had decided to cover the shame she felt for Neziah in having begot such greedy, snarling hyenas. She would hide, too, the wounds she had borne from her own son and from her father by concealing her identity. No one should know that such famous men had behaved so cruelly. Nor should they know her sense of outrage, not unmixed with self-pity. She would hold up her head and make some sort of life until she, too, was released by death. She decided to change her name. And vaguely aware of her mother's suffering, she called herself Mahalia.

"Sit here. I'll bring bread. Will you drink water? I have no wine. I am a poor widow, too. My name is Diklah."

The kind soul bustled about as she chattered. She made her guest eat and drink and then put her into a comfortable bed.

"You see I have too much house now that my children are gone abroad and my husband is dead—two courtyards, two big reception rooms. That was fine, for we were a big family and did much entertaining, but now really, there is no point in keeping it, but I don't know where else to go. Nobody wants to be burdened with the care of an old woman who has outlived her usefulness, you know."

"Yes, Diklah, I know," murmured Lily. She felt the comforting weight of the pouchpocket against her side and fell asleep. She had not slept a wink the night before, just sat on the rubble heap, torn between fear, anger, and bereavement.

Next morning the deal was quickly made. Lily would buy the house, Diklah would stay on to help with repairs and cooking. They both laughingly agreed that two women under the same roof was a recipe for trouble, but in their need it was worth a try.

Lily/Mahalia, relying on her experience at the Hanan homeplace, had a plan to establish a weaving business. She had had to handle transactions with suppliers in the Babylonian markets and was acquainted with the value and convenience of the recently introduced currency. Minted coins of established worth—many siglu—were readily calculated and pocketed by the businesswoman as she sold her jewels, bought wool and wood, and hired workmen.

Though she sought the most honest and reliable men—she had changed her sackcloth for braver garments—Lily knew that overall she was at a disadvantage and was frequently cheated. Short weight and skimped work left her helpless and angry because she could do nothing about it.

"Well," she said to Diklah with a sigh of resignation, if those rascals are so hard up that they have to rob widows, they can have their ill-gotten gains. Let it not be said that I pushed them into beggary."

"You mock, my friend Mahalia," the older woman answered, "but it is the common experience of all widows. I've heard many of them."

"Perhaps of all women without a husband, a son, or a father to stand up for them."

The two fell silent, reviewing their lives. "If only things had been different, if only she had made this choice instead of that. If only Lily had had a son by Neziah.

Mahalia was confirmed in her decision to make her weaving house a widow's resource. She told her plan to everyone who came within the sound of her voice: tradesmen, dyers, wool merchants, brick makers and masons, carpenters and vegetable hawkers.

"You'll end up feeding a lot of bums," laughed one young workman, "but I'll spread the word."

The first one to come was not a widow. She was a huge, ugly Babylonian woman, who said, "I want work. I know weaving. I work hard. I do not steal."

Mahalia showed her two looms set up in the brightest courtyard. The woman glanced carelessly at the one warped for the simple basket weave. She sat down before the smaller, lighter frame on which Lily had started an interesting twill in two shades of red. She examined the lisses, picked up a bobbin, and expertly continued the weft.

"Stay, by all means, and be one of us," sad Mahalia, forgetting about widowhood.

After supper Diklah came to her cubicle and told what she knew about their first weaver. She was named Amanu, the wife of the owner of the biggest textile factor in the city and also his foreman. She toiled all day at the looms and far into the night at domestic chores. She was worth her weight in gold.

"Maybe she won't stay long in this poor place," mourned Mahalia.

"Just long enough to copy your patterns," suggested Diklah.

Under questioning the next morning, Amanu stated firmly that she "worked in this place." She would not return to her husband, who had a taste

Exile

for sex with young girls. At first he had contented himself with fondling the women in his work rooms by day and coupling with them at night. Lately he had become more brazen—right out in the open, everybody could see. And laugh. It was not to be borne. Amanu was through!

Widows did come, some skilled, some not. Some came to reside, others in pleasanter circumstances went home at night. Mahalia bought more looms and undertook to sell on consignment the pieces of cloth made at home by women whose duties kept them there. She gave over the courtyard nearest the door to trade. The finished pieces were attractively displayed in the adjacent reception room. Discriminating dressmakers discovered the widow weavers, and ladies of taste appeared at court clad in shimmering fabrics, comparable to the silks of Cathay, at half the price."

By day Mahalia was the brisk, successful business woman. By night, she was Lily, who wept for her lost Neziah. He was gone. Where? She was alone. Why? How long would she have to suffer the consequences of her wrong turns and foolish desires? Through all the years of their happy, married life she had wanted a son. It was the right instinct, but it had been nullified by the years of secret lovemaking, and the fear, and the bitter herbs. Bitter, bitter, bitter repayment now and forever.

It was not all work and no play for Mahalia's widows. They talked endlessly about their lives, their children (all paragons), their impossible in-laws, their tastes in food and wine. And when dark came they quit their spindles and looms to listen to a talented one tell tales of the men and women of old, their ancestors who started at Yahweh's hands the human race. Those who by Yahweh's protecting wisdom survived the flood, and even of Abraham. He was the founder of their direct line, his sons Isaac and Jacob born later. But Abraham had started out right near here, at Ur of the Chaldees. Now that was a saga. And the long one about Moses, hidden in the bullrushes of the Nile who grew up to lead through many adventures, first up and then down. That man was a wonder, but he never got to the Promised Land. Joshua and all the judges. Those were thrilling times, so different from their humdrum lives in Babylon.

Sparkle was added to the monotony by the appearance of a singing woman named Naarah. She was tied at home caring for many grandchildren, and the cloth she brought for sale was far from the best. Recognizing her, Mahalia hung on her every word and encouraged her to come often and sing.

"I do crave a little adult conservation," said Naarah. "All day and all night those darling children, while their parents go gadding."

She did not recognize Lily in Mahalia. In fact, such had been the haze of her love for Ethan that she had no clear picture of Lily; just his mother, a shadow. After the abrupt departure, she had wondered vaguely if there might have been some interest there after all. The vagueness headed into nothingness as her and Ethan's affairs became more urgent. When she spoke of her family, she did not mention her mother-in-law, but was full of information about her famous husband, Ethan, and his equally famous grandfather Jeduthun.

"They knew all the praises of Israel, for Jeduthun had sung them in the Temple, as boy and man. He taught them to Ethan and me before I could feel their majesty. He said a voice called him to teach the children, and he did. So much effort in years of choir directing. They both made great and enduring poems out of the fullness of their hearts. I am sure you remember...." Naarah threw back her head, and out of her mouth came a stream of golden notes that left her hearers in silent awe.

> "I loved the Lord, because He hath heard my voice and my supplication.
> Because He hath inclined His ear unto me, therefore, I will call upon Him as long as I live.
> The sorrows of death encompass me, and the pains of hell got hold upon me: I found trouble and sorrow.
> Then called I upon the name of the Lord: O Lord, I beseech Thee, deliver my soul."[23]

Not all of Naarah's songs were from worship in the Temple: she had many gay ditties for dancing or for work in field and vineyard. To the delight of the weavers, she composed one for them that carried the count of the sheds and the beat of pressing home the weft.

"Rhythm, that's the way to measure time. My son, the astronomer at the Ziggurat, says up there they see the movement of the heavenly bodies and figure years and months. But I say for us below, we have to feel it in our bones, like a dance." Naarah demonstrated in three-quarter time, iambic as it was later known.

She gave them the beat and then the song, which they could adapt to different patterns, a help and a joy in their work:

> "Praise ye the Lord, our almighty creator. He gave us the loom and has threaded its warp. But we open the sheds and we pass through the shuttle and press down the weft of the fabric we weave, for the garment of life ...."

Naarah shook her graying head and laughed at herself. "I guess I sound like a preacher. You can change it for different patterns, but you get the idea; the beat, the rhythm."

The weavers agreed that it felt good to sing Naarah's song. They quickly learned it, and its possibilities for variation.

Needless to say, Naarah was the life of any gathering at which she appeared. Always on stage, mimic and actress, she fascinated her audience, be it one person or twenty. Lily was puzzled to know when she was serious or when she was making fun. She was more concerned about Ethan and Jeduthun, for sometimes Naarah spoke of them as if they were living, at other times as if they were dead. When pressed for a direct answer, Naarah's eyes would close and she would give some mystic utterances like: "Who knows but God?" Or, "Life. What is that? Death, but not buried?"

One day Naarah came to the weaving house and found Mahalia rippling a length of cloth and relishing the changing color as it responded to different angles of light.

"It is very beautiful," cried the singer. "Blue-green, green-blue. Or blue? Or green? Like the Lower Sea. Liquid emeralds."

"You have been to the Lower Sea?"

"Yes. I went there looking for Ethan."

"When was that?"

"Long ago. Long enough that the wound should have healed, but it has not." Naarah looked up piteously at the older woman.

Lily took her in her arms and the two women wept together.

Mahalia did not tell her that she was really Lily, Ethan's mother. She feared that past judgments of the two pillars of Naarah's life would put a strain on a treasured and growing friendship. Her silent embrace enabled Naarah to pour out her heart without embarrassment to one who had sympathetic understanding and more experience. The bond between the two women grew firmer and deeper because each gave what the other needed.

Little by little, Lily learned much, and Naarah found release in the telling. The search for Ethan had gone on for years. Nobody had seen, him since he left his grandfather at Nippur. Times were very unsettled, except in the walled towns; it was possible hat Ethan had met with violence. But who would harm a man so kind and generous and sweet as Ethan? Everybody liked him, and he liked everybody. Yes, the grandfather, Jeduthun had died not too long after Ethan vanished, before he could be questioned. There was still hope. No, Ethan's mother was not told, for she was no longer in the family. His father? He hadn't been heard from since he departed for Egypt during the siege. Of course lots of people came inquiring for Ethan; he was such a famous singer. But she could recall no one in particular.

Naarah's pent-up heart let Mahalia know further that, though always described as paragons of virtue and wisdom, her two boys left much to be desired as sons. It was the daughter, Alhai, whom Naarah held most dear and whose family were most needy of her loving care.

Alhai's husband, a good man, did not prosper, through bad luck or bad judgment, or both. His trade, sandalmaking, never brought in quite enough, and the family would have suffered real hardship if they had not had the help of Naarah. Naarah, herself, would have been unable to help without the legacy of Jeduthun, a bag of gold chains and rings brought to Ethan by his grandfather's friends in Nippur. Of course, Ethan never came home to see them, but Naarah knew he would want her to use them to provide for need in his absence.

Naarah was too proud to say such things directly, but Lily, no fool, inferred the situation. Confirmation came one day when Naarah visited, her wearing a little bracelet set with a blue stone.

She said, "I hate to sell this pretty bauble but I must. Would you like to buy it?"

Mahalia slipped the bracelet on her arm, admired it, but said she could not pay full value. Then suddenly she snatched it off. The blue stone had changed from the color of the sky to the brown of the great river, and the armband seemed to fasten itself around her arm, choking, suffocating.

"Get rid of it! Quickly! It is cursed!"

It seemed, too, that the once flourishing synagogue at Eleazar's house (for so they now called the gathering places) had fallen upon cursed times. With no one to make the music and only an occasional visiting priest to read the Word, there was no longer a regular Sabbath worship, and the congregation drifted away.

Naarah, fearing vandalism, had brought the scrolls home for safe-keeping. If Ethan returned... Meanwhile, she taught her grandchildren and their little friends the grand old praises that Jeduthun had taught her and Ethan.

---

[23] Psalms 116

Chapter 19
Bread upon the Water

One afternoon Naarah, entering the weavers' house, found it strangely quiet. Mahalia was in bed, and Diklah very much in charge of the patient, ordering the women around, forbidding company, quoting the doctor, and generally acting possessive. Over her protests, Naarah went up to the sick woman and saw her friend motionless and rigid. At the sound of Naarah's voice, she opened her eyes and struggled to speak but could not.

Mahalia had had an unexplained fall, after which her right side was paralyzed, and she had lost the power of speech. The weavers did what they could to make her comfortable. Doctors offered potions, which she would not drink. They said the best would be to keep the patient very quiet: no noise, no excitement, no decisions, no stress. Diklah took this to mean no company, even the favorite Naarah, of whom she was jealous anyway.

Naarah left quickly the first day, going home to think and pray. She returned the next day firmly resolved.

"Mahalia does not need bad things, but she does need good. I shall visit her every day, and you are not to make a fuss about it. I shall bring her happy talk, good news, quiet bits of family doings. She must not lie there as in a tomb. Let's give her a part in the life around hers."

Diklah shook her head but gave way to the superior status of the wife of the illustrious Ethan, the line of great Temple singers. And so Naarah came every day with a little song and a brief report on familiar scenes. Mahalia gave signs of enjoying family news. She tried to speak but could only make a hissing sound. She could move her left hand, however, and with Naarah's loving help developed a way of expressing herself.

Naarah would ask, "Shall I bathe your forehead?"

The left hand would move up and down to say yes, sideways to say no.

"Do you like this song?" The left hand would move to the heart to express enjoyment, or push away to signal distaste.

Thus they spent peaceful hours together. Mahalia did seem to rejoin the land of the living. All the weavers thought she improved.

Then came great stirrings, exciting news that roared through the Jewish communities in Babylonia and even shook the quiet backwater that was the Widows' House of Weavers. Two prophets openly proclaimed the end of

Rachel Stern

Babylon and the return of the exiles to their homeland. There was one, a highly placed but devout Hebrew, who was called on by the frivolous King Belshazzar to interpret portents that the wisest Chaldeans could not (or would not) understand. Daniel spoke out and told the king that Yahweh was going to destroy him for drinking out of the holy vessels of silver, looted from the temple by Nebuchadnezzar. It was quite a scene, according to swelling reports: giant fingers writing on the wall in the midst of revelry; Belshazzar, scared into a fit, calling for soothsayers, promising and threatening; Daniel, who at one time had proved Yahweh's power to Nebuchadnezzar, coming to tell the ruler of the greatest power on earth that he was a lightweight, unfit to reign, and would be finished off.

The tellers of this drama were not too sure of the facts, which they were perfectly willing to sacrifice for the sake of the story. And it was a good story, relished and repeated and embellished wherever the exiles gathered. The weavers, though, thought Mahalia should not be excited and simply whispered among themselves.

The second, more important prophet was substantial. He came out of obscurity and spoke at length, and often, of a powerful message from God, like that of Isaiah, whose scrolls, warning Israel of the coming doom under Sennacherib, were cherished and often read. He, too, carried hope of a Redeemer in years to come. But he also had a specific promise for the Chosen People: Cyrus, king of Persia, would conquer Babylon and release the captives to go home. Rumblings of war and uncertainty at the Babylonian court lent credence to this prophesy. Naarah thought that her family should be prepared. She needed to talk to her mentor about this. She thought and prayed.

Mahalia lay white and still. Naarah, looking down at her, imagined how beautiful she must have been when she was young. Aloud but softly, she said, "Mahalia, I bring you lilies."

The great dark eyes flashed open in welcome. She was pleased but, trying to speak, could make only that hissing noise. Naarah thought she wanted the lilies brought close. Mahalia pointed back and forth between the lilies and herself. Naarah gave up trying to understand, put the yellow and pink flowers in a jar, and sat beside the bed.

"I have a little bit of news for you, but I can's stay unless you are quiet."

Mahalia dutifully quit trying to convey her own message and listened to Naarah. She told of the coming of the great prophet with a message of hope for the captives.

"That is a very sweet hope for all of us. We should draw strength from the promise, and pray for its fulfillment. Sleep on it, dear friend. I'll see you tomorrow."

On the morrow, when she again looked down upon the invalid, she thought, "I wish I had known her in her youth. She is the kind of person one would choose as a companion on a long and toilsome journey."

Exile

As if reading her thoughts, Mahalia opened her eyes in glad recognition and made the affirmative motion with her left hand.

"Do you remember Jerusalem?"

Mahalia did.

"Was it very beautiful, a holy place to remember with pleasure?"

Mahalia was not only positive but also she carried her left hand to her heart.

"Think on these things, my dear. Good night. I'll be back tomorrow."

So little by little, Naarah learned that Mahalia approved of her plan to take the family home to Jerusalem. The planning, however, was easier than the execution. The elder son, the intellectual at the Ziggurat who had married a Babylonian, flatly refused to go. The second son, he was too well fixed in Babylon to want to move, but then there was the danger of losing his property in a war. On the other hand, he might make a still bigger fortune out of war profits. The daughter Ahlai and her husband quickly decided to return to the homeland. They left all the details of departure in Naarah's hands.

What to take and what to leave behind? There the difficulties piled up: "Mother, surely you are not leaving this fine chair." "Mother, it is foolish to take that old thing. Nobody has any use for it." "You haven't any sense at all about how to pack."

Naarah bit her lip and went on as best she could. Her elder son gave her a big wagon with a cover and two draft oxen. He would be glad to see the last of his odd family. His brother, finally deciding to remain under the benevolent rule of Cyrus, placated his conscience by giving his mother a two-wheeled cart and a donkey. She was thankful that she would not have to walk.

Gifts of food and clothing from neighbors piled up. Yet Naarah delayed the departure on account of Mahalia, who had developed a horrid cough and had refused food for days.

Naarah tried to feed her and cheer her up. She did not tell the sick woman that she was going, but brought her bits of song of the city of David, or from the Prophet, that she might be comforted.

> "Thou dost show us Thy good, Lord, and lift up the light of Thy countenance upon us.
>
> Thou has put gladness in our heart, more than in the time that their corn and their wine increased.
>
> I will both lay me down in peace, and sleep: for Thou, Lord, only makest me dwell in safety."[24]

Lily slept peacefully after this benediction; but, awakening within the confines of her paralysis, her mind raced out to the problems facing Naarah and the whole Jewish people. They shielded her, treated her like a child, but she overheard whispers and interpreted remarks. She wanted to shout, "Go, my children, with God's blessing. Do not let me hold you back!"

Another time Naarah brought the message voiced by Isaiah:

> *"Fear not, for I am with thee. Be not dismayed, for I am thy God;*
> *I will strengthen thee; Yea, I will help thee; Yea, I will uphold thee with the right hand of My righteousness."*[25]

"That should make us courageous to do His will, don't you agree, Mahalia?"

The old invalid signaled enthusiastic approbation, which persuaded Naarah to risk trying her own psalm the next day.

> *"When the Lord turned again the captivity of Zion, we were like them that dream.*
> *Then was our mouth filled with laughter, and our tongues with singing: then said they among the heathen, The Lord hath done great things for them.*
> *The Lord hath done great things for us; wherefore we are glad.*
> *Turn again our captivity. O Lord, as the streams in the South.*
> *They that sow in tears shall reap in joy.*
> *He that goeth forth and weepeth, bearing precious seed, shall doubtless come again with rejoicing, bringing his sheaves with him."*[26]

In the stillness of the night, Mahalia, rejoicing, slipped out of her mortal garment. It was laid to rest, by sheer chance, near the remains of her beloved, Neziah, in the heathen earth between the two rivers. Naarah and the weavers and the dirge. They allowed themselves a day of private mourning and then again took up their work.

"It is better to weave than weep," said Amanu.

---

[24] Psalms 4
[25] Isaiah 41
[26] Psalms 126

Chapter 20
The Chest

Naarah summoned her family and, brooking no argument, announced that they would pack the carts on the morrow and depart the day following. She ordered her son Sabtah, the entrepreneur who would try his luck with the Persians in need of shelter, to sell the two houses and send the proceeds through the banking firm of Hanan.

"Yes, Hanan. You heard me."

Alhai and her husband, Eber, would load and drive the big ox-drawn wagon. They would carry the looms, the beds, the cooking stones and vessels, and the bulkier provisions. Their eldest son, Darda, a tall lad of twelve, would drive the donkey cart and help his grandmother. The boy grinned at the prospect of beating the donkey, was less pleased at the prospect of listening to his grandma. They would buy goatskin replacements for their water jugs as soon as they reached the desert, where the tent dwellers made such things. Darda saw high adventure ahead.

The most valuable article to be carried in the donkey cart was the cedar chest, brought so carefully from Jerusalem. In it Naarah placed the scrolls entrusted to her and the few remaining musical instruments left by Ethan. As Darda and his brothers lifted the chest, Naarah saw incised on the bottom "Mahalia" and below that "Lily." The appearance of the names of its two previous owners stirred Naarah's memory, but in the rush of leaving, there was not time to speculate.

She said, "Lash it carefully. It is precious. Here, put these soft bundles around it. Darda, I'll tell you about this fine antique later."

Before sunup the next day, they were trundling across the Euphrates bridge, heading west and followed by the heavy-laden wagon. They passed the Hanan property without noticing an out of the city wall. Here they waited for the rest of the party to catch up. Naarah said she would take one of the smaller girls in her lap—if she'd be good. Then they turned northward within the watered crescent. Naarah began to sing her psalm.

> *"We shall come again rejoicing, bringing our sheaves with us. Children, do you know that within the chest the seed of music went to Babylon? Do you realize that we are taking home the*

> increase? It is as if the seed has been planted and tended and has borne grain. The tears of our exile watered it, seventy years of captivity among the heathen, and now we are happy that Yahweh has ended our punishment. He is sending us back to the land he gave our forefathers, that we may worship on His holy hill."

The two youngsters learned the song and enjoyed it whenever the way grew dull.

"Now, about the chest: It came into our family with Mahalia when she married Jeduthun, your great grandfather. Say it: Jeduthun was our great grandfather; Mahalia was his wife."

They repeated.

"Jeduthun was the most illustrious musician of his time, both in his Temple in Jerusalem and in the synagogues of Babylon. He later worked with the scribes to write all the recollections, and made copies of all the written records and literature of our nation, lest we lose our identity as the ten other tribes did."

"What are tribes?"

"Families, descendants of the sons of Jacob."

"Who is he?"

"Don't they teach you anything in school?"

After a long silence Naarah resumed, "Ethan..."

"Yes. I know about him. Our grandfather. He disappeared ...."

Naarah tried again, "There was a great lady in poverty who helped widows in the weaving house. She called herself Mahalia, but she was so interested in Ethan that I've wondered if there is some connection with Lily. That name means lilies, you know, and...."

"Aw, Grandmother, all those people are dead. And they were so old," protested the boy.

"Not always," replied the once-brilliant voice of his grandmother.

She fell silent, remembering her lost love. Where was he now? She needed his arms about her, needed to feel his presence at the journey's end. But she knew it could not be, and she shuddered to think of his body bereft of life in the mud of an alien land. She remembered his illustrious grandfather, Jeduthun, who loved the boy Ethan and poured all his hopes and dreams into him. Why had he been torn from their ancestral land and the Temple that nourished them? She could not remember Ethan's parents. She wondered and imagined. They, too, were lost. So much was lost in the land of their exile, even most of her living family. Why?

How could she sing that they turned homeward rejoicing, bringing sheaves? Sown in sorrow? Yes. Rejoicing? No. She knew that the Judean homeland was desolate, savaged, and that not one stone of Solomon's Temple was left standing. Yet she could not do otherwise than go home.

Exile

And so Naarah and her grandson jounced along in the cart, he excited by the adventure, she drawn irresistibly to the rock her fathers had known as home.

Behind them, they left the proud city that had conquered and been conquered, the luxurious high-built city, whose towers touched the sky and whose river nourished and enriched it; Babylon, the wicked, where people worshipped gods made with their own hands and prayed to them according to their own desires. Naarah knew that her people had left much of themselves in that heathen place, more than family and friends. Had that great Euphrates washed away their latent yearning after false gods and their dependence on the Temple as the one place of worship?

She felt this vaguely, instinctively, and she sensed, too, that she had a purpose in taking that chest of scrolls back to Jerusalem. She was not a priest or a scribe, learned in the law. She was a singer, a singer of the praises of Israel that held the remnant together for seventy years in a hard land of temptation. She could still sing and keep their hearts up. Let others come later with more resources to build and ordain—she could sing praises to Yahweh for her people.

And so it was that after the weary exiles had made camp, and after the sun they had faced all afternoon had set in a blaze of glory and the first cool stars were beginning to appear, Naarah took her lyre, and looking upward sang:

> *"The Lord is my light and my salvaiton. Whom shall I fear?*
> *The Lord is the strength of my life: of whom shall I be afraid?*
> *Hear, O Lord, when I cry with my voice; Have mercy also upon me, and answer me.*
> *When Thou saidst, seek ye My face, my heart said unto Thee, Thy face, Lord, will I seek."*[27]

Naarah's strong, high tones rose and vibrated as if she had found the face of her God. She carried her audience with her, and then she gently brought them down to earth.

> *"When my father and my mother leave me, then the Lord will take me up.*
> *Teach me the way, O Lord, and lead me in the plain path because of my infirmities.*
> *I had fainted unless I believed to see the goodness of the Lord in the hand of the living."*

She paused and swept the strings of her lyre for a moment, long enough to let the people think of their own needs. They were ready for the final message.

> *"Wait on the Lord; be of good courage, and He shall strengthen thine heart.*
> *Wait, I say, on the Lord."*[28]

A song of David reassured God's people that night, as in ages past and in ages yet to come.

---

[27] Psalms 27
[28] Psalms 27

Epilogue

Naarah's party joined others (some 50,000) who returned from Babylon to Jerusalem under Zerubbabel, the governor, and Joshua, the priest, in 536 B.C. They were beset by difficulties, but did manage to build the second Temple, a poor thing compared to the first. Since there were 200 singers in this first group of returnees, Naarah and her brood must have been in the choir.

In 457 B.C. Ezra, the scribe and priest, came from Babylon and to the aid his struggling countrymen, bringing precious documents and knowledge of the proper worship of Yahweh. Nehemiah came to regulate government and to rebuild the wall in 444 B.C. The restoration was completed under the enlightened rule of Darius.

The third Temple (of Jesus' time) was the spectacular gift of Herod the Great, the Roman appointed ruler of Jerusalem. It was demolished by the Romans in A.D. 70. On the site is the Dome of the Rock, a Muslim shrine, circa seventh century A.D.

Christian sacred places go back to the fourth century A.D., when Helena marked them for the Roman Emperor Constantine, her son. In the middle ages there was for one hundred years a kingdom of Jerusalem, guarded and ruled by Crusaders.

Recently, Babylonia has held our attention under its current name Iraq. The Lower Sea is, of course, the Persian Gulf.